This special
signed edition is limited
to 500 numbered copies
and 52 lettered copies.

This is copy _298_.

THIS IS RADIO CLASH

THIS IS RADIO CLASH

THIS IS RADIO CLASH

THIS IS RADIO CLASH

THIS IS RADIO CLASH

RADIO CLASH

is dead.
anybody know any better ones?

I WANT YOUR FUTURE

The Clash

NO HERO

I WANT

NO EXIT

I WANT

LABOUR ISN'T WORKING.

YOUR FUTURE

ROCK & ROLL

Radio CLASH

YOUR FUTURE

The Hour
Before Dawn

and Two Other Stories
from Newford

The Hour

Before Dawn

and Two Other Stories
from Newford

Charles de Lint

Subterranean Press ✳ 2005

First Edition

ISBN
1-59606-027-1

Subterranean Press
PO Box 190106
Burton, MI 48519

www.subterraneanpress.com

Contents

for Joe & Karen Lansdale:
bigger than life
but so down to earth

Author's Note

Ilove writing short stories — almost as much as I love reading them. I don't know how it is for other authors (and pardon me if you've heard me talk about this before), but for me it provides the chance to take risks, colour outside the lines, and follow my muse into a different kind of story (such as the one about the 50's private eye in the title piece of this collection). I'm like an artist playing with new media, colour and techniques, mixing first and third person points-of-view, say. Or mixing present and past tense. Or mixing them all.

If the experiment doesn't work out, I've only lost a week or two of work, as opposed to the sixteen months or so I need to put into a novel. But if it does work, then I have some new narrative tools to add to the bunch already jumbled up in the toolbox that sits somewhere in the back of my head.

Short stories are also a great place to catch up on a character from a novel. I might not want to spend a whole other book doing so (there are so many other characters' stories to tell), but I do enjoy checking in just to see how they're doing. Short stories are the perfect length to indulge myself in this, and that's how Miki Greer (from *Forests of the Heart*) ended up in "The Butter Spirit's Tithe."

*

Why these three stories?

For that you'll have to ask Bill Schafer (Mr. Subterranean Press) who called to say he wanted to publish this slim collection and suggested the ones you'll find herein. Well, actually, he suggested the first and third stories. I got to choose "That Was Radio Clash," one of my favorite stories from the past few years.

For one thing, it let me deal with the huge hole left by the death of Joe Strummer — at least it was a huge hole for me.

I didn't grow up on Strummer's music (either with the Clash, his brief stint with the Pogues, or in his last band the Mescaleros). My first musical touchstones came in the two decades before that. But from when the Clash burst on what felt like a stagnant music scene in the seventies, to the present day when Strummer is no longer with us, his music has remained a constant part of the soundtrack of my life.

"That Was Radio Clash" is also what I call a gift story. Most of the time, writing stories is five percent inspiration and ninety-five percent chipping away, paragraph by paragraph, line by line, sometimes word by word, to get it properly told. But every so often a story comes along with so little effort on my part that I feel as though I'm channelling it, typing madly away simply to catch the words as they come bubbling out of my head.

A gift, indeed.

Just like Strummer's music was to me.

*

If any of you are on the Internet, come visit my home page at www.charlesdelint.com.

Charles de Lint
Ottawa, late Autumn 2003

The Hour Before Dawn

Newford, September 1957

Let me tell you about the real witching hour: the hour before dawn when uninvited spirits come visiting. Ghosts, demons, any bodiless thing can come sliding into your dreams right about then. It's got something to do with it being the last dream of the night, but I'm not big on the details of the how or why. All I know for sure is, I don't much appreciate it. Personally, I want to talk to some dead guy, I'd rather call him up on my own dime. Pick the time and place, make sure I'm ready for the encounter, because I purely do hate surprises.

But the dead don't especially have much consideration for those of us who happen to not be deceased ourselves. Everybody gets visits from them, only most people don't remember like I do. And maybe the dead don't come to me every night—or at least I don't remember them coming every night—but I wake up far too often with the sour ache that they leave in my heart.

All of which is to explain why I wasn't particularly overjoyed at having a pleasant roll in the hay with Ginger Maloney be interrupted by the ghost of my ex-wife's sister-in-law.

Hell, I didn't even know Ina Bell had died.

Alive, she was no pretty thing; dead, she makes my skin crawl.

Imagine a woman about as wide as she is tall, hair like thin straw, two little dark eyes that get lost in the vast expanse of her piggy face. Now I know looks aren't everything. I've been with big women and they're not so different from the skinny ones. There's just more of them to hold. The real measure of a woman is what she's got inside and that's where Ina truly comes up short. She was about as self-centered and bitter as they come. Nobody ever did right by her — not in her book. If she ever had a kind word for anyone, I never heard it.

"Kind of pathetic," she says, once she's chased Ginger out of my head. "Making time with the widow of your own dead partner."

"It was a dream," I tell her. "You don't plan them. You just lie back and enjoy it and worry about the guilt later."

"Can't see you worrying about much of anything."

"Yeah, well, there's a lot you don't know."

"When it comes to you, I consider that a blessing."

I decide politeness has run its course.

"What do you want from me?" I ask.

"I want to know why I'm dead."

"How's that my problem?"

"You won't help?"

"Why should I?"

She shrugs. "It's the charitable thing to do? For old times sake? Simple curiosity? Take your pick."

"You know, I never much cared for you when you were alive and dead's not turning out to be much of an improvement."

"I guess that'd be a no."

"You'd be guessing right."

She gives me a slow nod. "Then it looks like you'll be seeing a lot more of me, Jack Daniels. Every morning, right around this time. You think about that."

"Now wait a minute—"

But she's already gone, the alarm clock's ringing, and I wake up on the sofa in my office with a bad taste in my mouth and that sour ache in my heart. I don't have any mouthwash, but I do have a pack of gum. I shove a stick in my mouth and chew until my mouth feels as clean as the magazine ads claim it should. Then I light up a cigarette and make a waste of all that chewing.

Making a waste of things is pretty much my specialty.

It's the reason I'm sleeping in my office. Couldn't hold my marriage together, but I don't make enough as a private dick to pay rent on more than my ex's apartment and this place, so I sleep here when office hours are over.

Right now, I don't have the stamina to call Ella and ask her about her sister-in-law, not without fortifying myself first. It's too early—even for me—to open the bottom drawer of my desk and have a nip from the bottle with my namesake on the label. Instead, I grab the kettle and head down the hall to the public washroom. I have a leak, shave and splash some water on my face. I'll go to the Y later for a shower.

Filling the kettle, I bring it back to my office and put it on the hot plate. Not until I have a cup of instant coffee and another cigarette going, do I pick up the phone and dial the number of my old apartment.

"Yeah?" Ella answers with her usual charm.

Time was she was the sweetest thing, but then once upon a time, things were different for all of us. Tom was still alive and Korea hadn't left its mark on either of us. I guess Ella had her own troubles, but she never talked about them, and I never asked, which I guess tells you everything you need to know about why our marriage took a nose dive and never recovered. Ginger's the only one who didn't change so much, though after Tom died, a sadness slipped into her eyes and it just never went away.

The guilt I told Ina I'd be feeling shows up right about then, but I manage to put it aside. The dead that come visiting me in my dreams might be real, but nothing else is.

"I just heard about Ina," I say to my ex.

"Funeral's over, and so's the wake. So you're going to have to look somewhere else for free booze."

"Nice."

"Hey, I didn't drink *my* way out of a job."

I didn't mean to, I want to say. I just needed something to get the damn voices in my head to shut up. Turned out I really needed to listen to them instead.

"I didn't call to fight," I tell her.

"That's new. So why did you call?"

"I wanted to find out what happened to Ina."

She sighs. "Jesus, Jack. Why do you even pretend to care?"

"I don't…I mean…"

My voice trails off and I can imagine the look on her face from the cold silence that falls between us.

"I don't ask for them to come to me," I say.

"'Course you don't."

"It's just—"

"What you need to do is go see a shrink," she says. "But I guess that's too much to ask from a big tough guy like you."

"All a shrink's going to do is…"

I don't bother to finish because she's already hung up on me. I drop the handle onto the receiver and go downstairs to the newsstand to get myself a paper and some breakfast at Nick's Diner down the block. I hardly have time to sit down in a booth before Judy's coming over with a plate of bacon and eggs and a cup of joe. She's another of those big women, but unlike Ina, she's got a smile and kind word for everyone.

I spread the paper out on the table. The front page has more on the mess in Little Rock. Faubus has gone ahead and sent in the National Guard to stop nine

Negro kids from entering the city's Central High School. I just shake my head.

About the one thing I brought back from Korea was the realization that it doesn't matter what we look like. Under our skin, we're all the same. We all bleed the same red blood.

The paper doesn't say what Ike's going to do, but the ball's in his court now and I sure as hell hope he doesn't fumble it.

I turn to the local pages and then the obits as I eat my breakfast. I don't really expect to find anything about Ina in there — if she's already in the ground, any news on how she died would have been reported earlier. I'm just wondering if anybody else I know's kicked the bucket. I don't see any familiar names.

Thinking about Ina reminds me how there was nothing much when Tom died, either. But that's the way it is with the little people. Unless we go out in a particularly spectacular way, it's not news. It doesn't mean anything, except to those of us left behind to pick up the ruin of our lives.

Why'd Tom eat his gun? Nobody seems to have an answer, but I know.

He was always talking about the state of the world. I remember not long before he went into the garage and put his old service pistol in his mouth, he told me, "I can't stop thinking how the world's such an ugly place. And every time you're sure that this is as bad as it's going to get, things just seem to get worse."

I knew he was really talking about Korea, about what we did there, the killing. About what was done to us. About what the killing made of us.

I don't think anybody who goes to war can ever really let it go. Those first few weeks you're home, they treat you like a hero. But eventually you have to live with the memories you've got sitting in your head.

And what good did we really do? It wasn't over. War's never over. It sits on the borders of civilization, hungry and waiting. The Ruskies sure as hell aren't going to back down. The Cold War's going to heat up—anybody can see it coming. Next time it'll be atomic bombs and what little we've still got that's good in the world will all be destroyed.

That's why Tom ate his gun. But how do you tell his widow that? How do you tell anyone? Nobody wants to hear that kind of stuff. We're supposed to deal with what the world throws at us. Only cowards take the easy way out.

Except I think it's more complicated than that. Hell, I know it is. I've got the stories the dead tell to back me up, but people *really* don't want to hear about that.

I finish my breakfast and head off to the Y for my shower, then I ride the streetcar to Upper Foxville.

I'm chasing down a bail-jumper for Tony Vario who runs a bail bond office out of a storefront on Palm Street. He's got a regular crew to collect the no-shows, but every once in a while he throws me a bone. He figures he owes me for saving his kid back in

Korea. It's something I would have done anyway, but these days I don't turn down the work.

Joseph Miller's not to hard to track down. I find him at his mother's place on MacNeil and he only puts up a token fight. He doesn't really want to get into it — we've got the same height, but he's a stringbean and I'm at least twice his size. But he's got his pride, I guess.

I drop him off at the Crowsea precinct, fill in the paperwork and I'm done until later tonight when I have a husband to follow.

It's kind of funny. I got screwed over by the courts, but here I am all the same, collecting evidence that'll put some other poor chump in the same boat. Except I never cheated on Ella. I just agreed to the divorce because it was easier than arguing with her about it.

With time on my hands, I decide to drop in on Frank Bell, Ina's husband. Or I guess I should say widower now.

Frank meets me at the front door of the little clapboard house he and Ina bought back in '49 before the prices started going up. He looks smaller than I remember. I offer him my hand.

"I only just heard about Ina," I say. "I wanted to come by and give you my condolences."

Frank doesn't speak, but his eyes well with tears and the next thing you know, the tears are streaming down his cheeks. He just stands there, shoulders drooping, crying.

I don't know what to do. What are you supposed to do when a guy just starts crying on you? But I know I have to do something. So I pat him awkwardly on the shoulder and then steer him back into the house, closing the door behind us.

I make us coffee and sit through a couple of smokes while he gets himself together.

"It's hard," he finally says. "I don't know what to do without her." He lifts his gaze to mine. "I guess...I guess the hardest thing is how people think I should just be...relieved. Like living with Ina was some kind of hardship."

I try to think of a diplomatic way to put it and settle for, "She didn't exactly go out of her way to make people comfortable."

That actually gets the hint of a smile twitching on his lips.

"Yeah," he says, "she was a spitfire, all right."

"So what happened?" I ask.

"She died in her sleep. I just woke up and...she was gone."

"Jesus."

Tears well in his eyes again, but this time he holds them back.

Neither of us say anything for a long moment. I'm trying to work my way around what he's just told me. I know enough from the visits that the dead pay me to know that they're usually aware of how they died, so there's no big mystery here for Ina. Why'd she die? It just happened. Her time was up.

"Do you think she had, you know, any unfinished business?" I ask.

Frank gives me a puzzled look. "What do you mean?"

"I don't know. Sometimes when people go before their time, there are important things that they've left undone. Things that were important to them, anyway."

"I'd guess everybody must leave unfinished business, then," Frank says. "But with Ina…well, she wasn't shy about letting people know where they stood in her esteem, so I guess she'd be about as ready as any of us when our time comes."

I nod.

"I'll tell you a mean thought I've had since she died," Frank says. "I wish it'd been me that went first so I didn't have to feel this pain. But then I think of Ina on her own, and I can't really wish this hurt on her."

"You got along well?"

He looks surprised. "We were soul mates, Jack."

I need to work through that as well. It's something you tend to forget: everybody's got someone who loves them, even if it's only their mother.

"Why are you asking about unfinished business?" Frank wants to know.

I shrug and try to think of a way to answer his question without having to get into Ina's visit this morning. But he seems to be way ahead of me.

"She came to you, didn't she?" he says. "She's been one of your morning visitors."

I just look at him.

"They used to come to Ina, too," he explains, "except she couldn't do much to help them. Not the way she said you do — you know, working out their leftover problems for them and everything. All she could do was give them a sympathetic ear."

"You don't think this is crazy?" I have to ask. "Ella thinks I should be seeing a shrink about it."

He shakes his head. "It's what Ina told me and she'd never lie to me — not about this. Not about anything. Like I said, we were close."

"And you're okay with the idea of the dead hanging around like this?"

"I don't know that I'd like it happening to me — not unless it was Ina coming to visit."

Yeah, well, dead, she's no charmer, I want to tell him. But then for him, that probably wouldn't be true.

"You get used to it," I say.

"So what did she say to you?"

He's so eager, I hate to let him down.

"Not a lot. She just wants me to find out why she's dead."

"I'd like to know that myself," he says.

I nod, though I hadn't taken her asking to be particularly philosophical. I'd figured there was some question as to how she'd died, like she'd been murdered, but never got to see who did it. But now that I've talked to Frank, I really don't know what she wants. Just to bring me some misery, I suppose.

I stand up.

"Well, if I figure it out," I tell Frank, "I'll let you know."

"Tell her I love her."

"From what you've told me, I'm sure she knows that."

"Tell her anyway. It's not something you can hear too often."

"I will," I say.

Turns out the husband I follow that night is definitely cheating on his wife. I want to give him a break — go up to him and tell him not to screw this up — but I need the money and it's not like anyone's forcing him to do it. So I take my pictures and drop the film round to Eddie's. He'll have a full set of glossies for me by tomorrow afternoon that I can give to the wife, along with my bill.

I'm tempted to stop in at the corner bar when I leave Eddie's, but I go back to the office instead. I turn on the radio and listen to Benny Goodman playing at a ballroom somewhere, where people are out having fun instead of lying on the sofa in their office, staring up at the ceiling and smoking cigarettes. I think about the bottle in the bottom drawer of my desk, but I don't touch it either.

I'm feeling virtuous, if lonely as hell, when I finally fall asleep.

*

Right before dawn, Ina shows up again. This time I'm not dreaming of Ginger. I'm just standing under an awning, watching the rain come down on the street in front of me, when she appears beside me, taking up way too much space.

"So," she says. "You learn anything, or is our meeting like this every morning going to be a regular habit?"

"Face it, Ina," I tell her. "The only why to your being dead is that the world just got sick of all your bitching and moaning and pulled the plug on you."

But I'm only mouthing the words out of habit. After my visit with Frank, I don't feel the same annoyance towards her anymore. I figure, anybody who can have such a close and loving relationship with their husband…well, they've got more good points going for them than maybe I can see.

I turn to look at her. "There's no mystery to it, no unfinished business. Your number just came up."

"So you were talking to Frank?"

I nod.

"How's he doing?"

"He misses you. Asked me to tell you he loves you."

Ina sighs. "I miss him, too."

"He told me the dead used to come see you."

"Yeah, but I could never do much for them, so I used to send them to people like you."

"Thanks a lot."

"You've got what it takes to help them," she says.

I shake my head. "Why do you think that is? Why do they come to me?"

"You're like a light — somebody they know is going to pay attention and maybe even help them deal with whatever leftover crap that's keeping them from moving on. They all talk about you, over here on the other side."

"Yeah? How come Tom never came to me?"

"I'm guessing he didn't have any unfinished business."

"Not like you."

She smiles. "What makes you think I came back for me? Maybe I came back for you."

"What the hell's that supposed to mean?"

"Look what you've done with your life, Jack. You're no more alive than Tom is."

That hit too close to home.

"Yeah? Why should you care?"

"Why shouldn't I?"

"Oh, for —"

"We never got along," Ina says, interrupting, "and that's okay. I didn't make it easy for you. But I don't make it easy for anybody. So maybe I didn't show it, but I always liked you, Jack."

"Right. That's why we got along so well."

"I told you, that's just the way I was. But see, I've got to give you this, Jack. Any hard words you had for me had nothing to do with the way I looked. And more important, to me, you never ragged on Frank for 'marrying that fat ugly mountain' as his own father told him one time."

"I always liked Frank," I tell her, just to be saying something. "Don't know how he put up with that mouth of yours, but I figured it was his business."

Ina grins. "That mouth's what kept me sane. Best defense is offense."

"I suppose."

"Christ, Jack. Look at me. Nobody was going to buy sweetness and light coming out of something like me."

"I think you're selling yourself short."

"You didn't grow up being me."

I nod. "But the folks that treated you hard, they weren't worth knowing anyway."

"Even my own family?"

"Even your own family," I tell her. "Maybe especially them, since they should've stood by you instead of jumping on the bandwagon. But maybe you could have laid back a little on the harsh words— you might've made some friends."

"And you'd be first in line, I suppose."

"Why not?"

"Maybe…hell, you're probably right. And if I'll admit to that, will you at least think about what I've been saying?"

"Sure. Am I going to see you again?"

"That all depends on you, Jack."

And then she's gone, and so is the rainy street. I'm back in my office again and I hear somebody unlocking the front door.

Damn, I forgot it was Saturday.

I sit up quick. I run a comb through my hair, try to straighten my shirt, but there's no way I can disguise that I was sleeping in my clothes and that I'm just waking up.

And in walks Ginger.

Back when Tom was still alive, when we still ran the agency together, Ginger would come in on Saturdays and work on some of the paperwork that had built up over the week—filing, receipts, invoices. We weren't taking advantage of her—she got a salary, the same as us. But after Tom died and my marriage went down the tubes, there wasn't enough work and I couldn't afford even the little I was paying her, so I had to let her go. Except she keeps coming in anyway, over my protests. Every Saturday, regular as clockwork.

There were long silences at first—not because of any bad feelings between us. We just didn't have anything to talk about that didn't leave one or the other feeling sad, or angry. Then, slowly, we started talking again—but never about personal stuff. She pretends not to notice that I'm living here in the office. She doesn't say anything about how I've let the business slide, how now I'm working on making a complete ruin of the rest of my life. She doesn't have to. I know all too well what's happening.

The problem is, I can't seem to stop it. When I get a job, I do it, and I do it well. But I'm not hustling for work, and when I'm not working, most of the time I just sit here in the office and stare at the walls. I don't think about eating my gun. Truth is, I don't think about much of anything at all. I listen to the big bands on the radio. I smoke my cigarettes. I drink my instant coffee. I go out to eat when I've got some money. When I don't, I heat something on the hot plate and eat it out of the can.

Ina's right. It's not living. But knowing you've got a problem and knowing how to fix it are two different beasts.

Ginger smiles at me when she comes in.

"Good morning, John," she says.

She's the only one who calls me by my given name. When I was a kid, some wag thought it was funny to call me Jack to go with the whiskey, and the nickname's pretty much stuck to me ever since.

"Morning," I say. "There wasn't much business this week, so there's not really anything to file."

I've long since given up trying to talk her out of these weekly visits. I mean, I feel bad having her come in, do some tidying and filing and I can't even pay her, but to tell you the honest to God truth, her showing up here every Saturday morning's pretty much the only thing I've got to look forward to. And isn't that a goddamned sorry state of affairs?

"That's all right," she says. "It gets me out of the apartment."

I nod. I wish I could say something to her, something personal, something that would let us connect, but all I can do is grab my shaving kit and ask her to excuse me for a minute.

I shave, wash up. By the time I get back, she's made us each a cup of coffee. She's sitting in the straight-backed wooden chair by the desk where clients do when I actually have them. We chat a little about the business in Little Rock, how Ike's sent in federal troops to deal with the mob of white agitators that had gathered outside the school. I like that she's up on current events. She can talk arts, too, but I keep my mouth shut then because what do I know about art? But I like to listen to her, the sound of her voice, and we have the same tastes in music—definitely jazz.

All too soon it's twelve o'clock and she's leaving. I almost ask her if she wants to go grab some lunch, but I stop myself. Ina's visit has my head churning with crazy thoughts, thinking I should reach out, start living. But who are we kidding? I wouldn't wish myself on anybody—especially not Ginger—so I let her leave without saying anything.

After she's gone, I walk over to the diner for a late breakfast, then pick up the photos from Eddie's. They're crisp and clear, showing the poor chump on his way into a motel room with his arm around this gal in a tight skirt. By the time Mrs. John Wellington arrives at my office to pick up them and my report I'm in a bad enough mood that I don't even feel sorry for the husband. Mrs. Wellington is older than the woman in my pictures but she's still a looker with a nice way about her and her husband's an idiot for having an affair.

I have supper at the diner, alone. I think of going to a bar, maybe catch some music at one of the clubs on Grasso Street, but instead I head over to Jimmy's

Billiards on Palm and shoot a few games before coming back to the office and falling asleep to the sounds of Lester Young on the radio.

*

I'm standing on the Kelly Street Bridge, looking down at the water, when Ina shows up and I realize I'm dreaming. And before you ask, no, I wasn't thinking of taking a dive. I just like watching the movement of water. I've spent whole afternoons, sitting on a bench on the boardwalk by the Pier, just watching the lake, the ferries crossing over to Wolf Island.

"That the best you can do with Ginger?" she asks. "Talk about the civil rights movement and Bud Powell?"

I don't even turn to look at her.

"Why don't you go visit Frank," I say.

"I do. Every morning since I died. But he never remembers when he wakes up."

"How's that make you feel?"

She laughs. "What are you now, a shrink?"

"I think maybe Ella's right. Maybe I could use one."

"You're not crazy, Jack."

"Tell that to Ella."

"You just didn't talk about this with the right person."

I think about my conversation yesterday with Frank.

"When did you first start talking to the dead?" I ask her.

She shrugs. "It feels like all my life, but I guess it started in high school."

"For me it was after I got back from Korea — when I joined the NPD."

"That's right," she says. "You were a cop before you went into business with Tom."

I nod. "And then he upped and killed himself."

"Everybody dies," she says. "Just like everybody gets to talk to the dead. It's only that most people don't remember when they wake up in the morning."

"I wonder how we got picked."

Ina shrugs. "Who knows?"

"And you never told anybody but Frank?"

"Who was I supposed to tell? I never had any friends. No one likes to spend time with the ugly fat girl. Was I supposed to add crazy to my job description?"

"But Frank was okay with it? He didn't think you were nuts?"

She shakes her head. "We trusted each other. Completely. If I said something was happening…when I told him what I was dreaming, and how I knew the dreams were true, he believed me."

I nod. "I didn't really believe it myself until I first helped one of the dead. This guy just kept bugging me, morning after morning, until I finally went to the *Journal*'s morgue and looked up his story, and sure enough, everything he said was true, but I'd never met him before in my life. Never even heard of him before."

"So you fixed his problem."

"Yeah. It wasn't a big deal. He had some bonds stashed away in his garage and he wanted to make sure his wife got them." I smile, remembering. "It felt pretty good, helping them out. Both of them — the living and the dead."

"I couldn't do much for them except listen to their stories," Ina says. "Looking like I do, it wasn't so easy to get around or talk to people."

"Not to mention how you'd tear a strip off anybody who happened to open his mouth around you."

"You need to let that go," she says. "I'm not in your world anymore, so none of that matters."

"Except if you'd talked to people the way you're talking to me right now, maybe you'd have made some friends."

"Sure," Ina says. "So I was a bitch and you've got no life. Can we move on?"

But it was just such a goddamn waste, I want to say. Because I find myself genuinely liking her now, like I never did when she was alive. Get her smiling, get that pissed off look out of her eyes, and it turns out she's got a sweetness to her that I never got to see before. But she's right. There's no point in going on about it. She's dead and the chance to live differently is gone, too.

"So you only ever talked to Ella about it?" Ina asks.

I shake my head. "I told Tom, too. Not that I thought they were real—just that I was having these dreams."

"What did he have to say?"

"Nothing much. I guess he was too busy dealing with his own demons."

"Yeah, and we saw where that took him."

"What's that supposed to mean?"

"Nothing," she says. "Except you might as well have stuck the end of a pistol in your own mouth because you haven't really been living since then either."

"I thought we agreed to let that go."

She smiles. "No, we're just not talking about what-might-a-beens when it comes to me. My time is done. But you're still breathing, even if you're not living. You've still got a chance to turn things around."

"How'd you ever find out about the dead coming to me anyway?"

"Ella talked about it to Frank when you first told her."

"And he told you."

"We didn't have any secrets between us," Ina says.

"Yeah, well, look how well that worked with Ella and me."

"You just need the right person to confide your secrets to."

"Like you."

She shakes her head. "No, somebody living. Somebody you care about and who cares about you."

"That animal doesn't exist in my world."

"So now Ginger's an animal?"

"Jesus, Ina," I say. "Ginger's the last person I'd tell."

"And why's that?"

"She's already witness to how I've screwed up my life. I don't want her thinking I'm crazy on top of that."

"Except maybe knowing will explain to her how a still young, good-looking guy like you feels he's got to push the world away."

"Yeah, and maybe it won't."

"You won't know unless you try," Ina says. "What've you got to lose?"

"Everything."

Ina laughs. Not meanly, but it cuts all the same.

"If what you've got is everything," she says, "then you're even worse off than I thought."

And then she's gone and I'm waking up on the sofa in my office.

Ina's got me so frustrated, I feel like hitting something. Instead, I bundle up some clean clothes and head down to the Y. When I leave the Y, I'm freshly scrubbed, wearing a suit, white shirt and tie. The suit's a little wrinkled, but it's the best I've got. I stop back at the office and drop off my old clothes, then take the streetcar to Lewis Street. By the time I'm standing in the hall outside Ginger's apartment, I've got this shaky feeling in the pit of my stomach that I haven't felt since Korea.

If Ginger's surprised to find me standing there when she answers the door, she doesn't show it. She invites me in and asks if I'd like a coffee. We make small talk while the coffee percolates in this little aluminum pot she puts on the stove. I get up and pour us each a mug when it's done its job. I add a splash of milk to hers, then sit back down at the kitchen table. Finally, I light another cigarette and start to talk.

I tell her about how the dead come to me in dreams; how they showed up after Tom and I got back from Korea and I joined the NPD while he started the agency that's now mine; how I found if I drank enough they'd stay away and I wouldn't hear the echo of their voices inside my head all day; how the combination of telling Ella about my dreams, the drinking, and losing my job on the force killed our marriage; how after Tom took me in as a partner, I figured out that the dead were real and I could help them.

I run out of steam around then and light a cigarette from the butt of the one I'm smoking. I grind the butt out in the saucer we're using as an ashtray.

"Did Tom see them, too?" Ginger asks. "These dead people?"

I shake my head. "I don't think so. At least not so's he ever told me."

"That's one thing you're both good at," she says. "Not talking."

I don't know how to respond to that so I don't say anything, which proves her point, I guess.

"Why are you telling me this now?" she asks.

"I...I just thought you should know."

"But why now? Why wait four years to talk about this? Did it never occur to you how it'd be for me, watching you flush your life down the toilet like this?"

"I told Ella," I say, "and look where that got me. She thinks I should be seeing a shrink."

"I'm not Ella."

"Jesus, I know that."

"And I don't think you're crazy."

"You don't?"

She shakes her head. "No. It explains a lot. I always knew there was something going on with you, something strange. I could just never figure out what."

"Well, now you know my sorry secret."

"I guess I do," she says and then she sighs. "I thought we were close," she adds, her voice soft. "Sometimes I thought...that maybe we could be more than friends."

"That's why I'm telling you."

She gives a slow nod. That sad look Tom left in her eyes looks deeper than ever. She leans across the table and then before I can stop her, she slaps me hard in the face.

I jerk back.

"Jesus!" I say. "What was that for?"

"For waiting until now to talk to me about all of this."

"But—"

"And now I think you should leave."

"Come on, Ginger."

She's looking down at the table and shakes her head.

"Please," she says, refusing to lift her gaze. "Just go."

So I do.

I get as far as the hall outside her apartment and then I lean on the door. I feel about as bad as I've ever felt. Through the door, I can hear Ginger crying. I feel like crying myself, but I push away from the door and shuffle down the hall.

I want a drink bad, but I just walk the streets for a long time instead.

I have an appointment in the morning with a dead woman. To keep it, I need to be sober.

*

I'm waiting for Ina in my office at the hour before dawn. I've never been able to do this before, never knew I could: choose where I'll be when I'm dreaming. Be waiting for the ghost to show up.

I don't see her arrive. I just hear the weight of her settling into my client's chair and lift my gaze from my desk to find her sitting there, looking at me.

"That was a nice piece of advice you gave me," I tell her.

It's funny. I've been pissed off at her all night, but now that she's sitting here in front of me, I don't have it in me to tell her off like I was planning to. Guess you need a heart for that, but I left mine broken in the hall outside of Ginger's apartment. Or maybe I dropped it on one of the streets I was out walking last night.

"What happened?" she asks.

I tell her and she shakes her head the way you do when you've heard something so dumb, you can't believe you heard it.

"Did you tell her you were sorry?" she asks.

"Sure, I explained how—"

"Did you actually use the words 'I'm sorry?'"

"I don't know. I must have. But she—"

"Listen to me, Jack," she says. "Nobody wants to hear excuses and explanations. All they want is for you to admit you screwed up, for you to say you're sorry and it won't happen again. All that other crap can wait for another time."

"But—"

"Trust me on this, Jack. If you honestly believe you messed up, just tell her that. Tell her you're sorry and it won't happen again. And then shut your mouth."

"She already told me she doesn't want to see me again."

"Really? I thought she just asked you to leave."

"What's the difference?"

"Don't be more of an idiot than you already are," Ina says. "You go back to her and tell her you're sorry. Bring her some flowers—there should still be asters growing in my garden. Pick a bunch for her. And tell Frank I'm getting ready to move on, but I plan to be waiting for him wherever it is we go to next."

"Just like that," I say.

"Oh, it won't be easy. Saying you're sorry and meaning it—that's never easy, Jack. But if the other person means anything to you, it's worth it."

"What if she won't talk to me?"

"You won't find that out sleeping on your sofa, talking to some dead woman."

"I guess." I wait a beat, then ask, "You're really heading on?"

She nods. "I've done all I can here."

"You've..?"

"The dead aren't always looking for somebody to help them," she says. "Sometimes we stick around because there's someone *we* can help."

And then she's gone again.

*

Ginger works at the First Newford Bank on Williamson. She gets off around four. She's usually home by four-thirty, quarter to.

I've been sitting on the front steps of her apartment building since ten past four, holding a bouquet of the little purple flowers I picked in Ina's yard, when I finally see her coming down the street, blonde-red hair bobbing, that little sway in her hips when she walks. She stops on the pavement in front of me, but she doesn't say a word.

I stand up and offer her the flowers.

"I'm sorry," I tell her. "I've been an idiot and I'm truly sorry."

She holds my gaze with hers, searching.

I feel explanations and excuses pushing around in my brain, desperate to get out.

But, "And no matter what," I say, "I promise it won't happen again."

She makes me wait another long moment until finally the ghost of a smile twitches at the corner of her mouth. She takes the flowers and then my hand.

"Come on," she says and starts up the stairs, giving my hand a tug. "Let's see what we can put together for supper."

That Was Radio Clash

December 23, 2002

"Why so down?" the bartender asked the girl with the dark blue hair.

She looked up, surprised, maybe, that anyone had even noticed.

At night, the Rhatigan was one of the last decent live jazz clubs in town. The kind of place where you didn't necessarily know the players, but one thing the music always did was swing. There was none of your smooth jazz or other ambient crap here.

But during the day, it was like any other low-end bar, a third full of serious drinkers and no one that looked like her.

"Joe Strummer died yesterday," she said.

Alphonse is a good guy. He used to play the keys until an unpaid debt resulted in some serious damage to his melody hand. He can still play, but where he used to soar, now he just walks along on the everyday side of genius with the rest of us. And while maybe he can't express the way things feel with his music anymore, the heart that made him one of the most generous players you could sit in with is still beating inside that barrel chest of his.

"I'm sorry," he said. "Was he a friend of yours?"

The hint of a smile tugged at the corner of her mouth, but the sadness in her eyes didn't change.

"Hardly," she said. "It's just that he was the heart and soul of the only band that matters and his dying reminds me of how everything that's good eventually fades away."

"The only band that matters," Alphonse repeated, obviously not getting the reference. In his head he was probably running through various Monk or Davis line-ups.

"That's what they used to call the Clash."

"Oh, I remember them. What was that hit of theirs?" It took him a moment, but then he half-sang the chorus and title of "Should I Stay or Should I Go."

She nodded. "Except that was more Mick Jones's. Joe's lyrics were the ones with a political agenda."

"I don't much care for politics," Alphonse said.

"Yeah, most people don't. And that's why the world's as fucked up as it is."

Alphonse shrugged and went to serve a customer at the other end of the bar. The blue-haired girl returned her attention to her beer, staring down into the amber liquid.

"Did you ever meet him?" I asked.

She looked up to where I was sitting a couple of bar stools away. Her eyes were as blue as her hair, such a vibrant colour that I figured they must be contacts. She had a pierced eyebrow — the left — and pale skin, but by the middle of winter, most people have pretty much lost their summer colour. She was dressed like she was auditioning for a black and white movie: black jersey, cargos and boots, a grey sweater. The only colour was in her hair. And those amazing eyes.

"No," she said. "But I saw them play at the Standish in '84."

I smiled. "And you were what? Five years old?"

"Now you're just sucking up."

And unspoken, but implied in those few words was, You don't have a chance with me.

But I never thought I did. I mean, look at me. A has-been trumpet player who lost his lip. Never touched the glory Alphonse did when he played — not on my own — but I sat in with musicians who did.

But that's not what she'd be seeing. She'd be seeing one more lost soul with haunted eyes, trying to drown old sorrows in a pint of draught. If she was in her teens when she caught the Clash at the Standish, she'd still only be in her mid- to late-thirties now, ten years my junior. But time passes differently for people like her and people like me. I looked half again my age, and shabby. And I knew it.

No, all I was doing here was enjoying the opportunity for a little piece of conversation with someone who wasn't a drunk, or what she thought me to be: on the prowl.

"I knew him in London," I said. "Back in the seventies when we were all living in squats in Camden Town."

"Yeah, right."

I shrugged and went on as though she hadn't spoken. "I remember their energy the most. They'd play these crap gigs with speakers made out of crates and broomstick mike stands. Very punk—lots of noise and big choppy chords." I smiled. "And not a hell of a lot of chords, either. But they already had a conscience—not like the Pistols who were only ever in it for the money. Right from the start they were giving voice to a whole generation that the system had let down."

She studied me for a moment.

"Well, at least you know your stuff," she said. "Are you a musician?"

I nodded. "I used to play the trumpet, but I don't have the lip for it anymore."

"Did you ever play with him?"

"No, I was in an R&B cover band in the seventies, but times were hard and I ended up living in the squats for awhile, same as him. The closest I got to playing the punk scene was when I was in a ska band, and later doing some Two-Tone. But the music I loved to play the most was always jazz."

"What's your name?"

"Eddie Ramone."

"You're kidding."

I smiled. "No, and before you ask, I got my name honestly—from my dad."

"I'm Sarah Blue."

I glanced at her hair. "So which came first?"

"The name. Like you, it came with the family."

"I guess people who knew you could really say they knew the Blues."

"Ha ha."

"Sorry."

"'sokay."

I waited a moment, then asked, "So is there more to your melancholy than the loss of an old favourite musician?"

She shrugged. "It just brought it all home to me, how that night at the Standish was, like, one of those pivotal moments in my life, only I didn't recognize it. Or maybe it's just that that's when I started making a lot of bad choices." She touched her hair. "It's funny, but the first thing I did when I heard he'd died was put the eyebrow piercing back in and dye my hair blue like it was in those days — by way of mourning. But I think I'm mourning the me I lost as much as his passing."

"We can change our lives."

"Well, sure. But we can't change the past. See that night I hooked up with Brian. I thought he was into all the things I was. I wanted to change the world and make a difference. Through music, but also through activism."

"So you played?"

"Yeah. Guitar — *electric* guitar — and I sang. I wrote songs, too."

"What happened?"

"I pissed it all away. Brian had no ambition except to party hearty and that whole way of life slipped into mine like a virus. I never even saw the years slide away."

"And Brian?"

"I dumped him after a couple of years, but by then I'd just lost my momentum."

"You could still regain it."

She shook her head. "Music's a young person's game. I do what I can in terms of being an environmental and social activist, but the music was the soul of it for me. It was everything. Whatever I do now, I just feel like I'm going through the motions."

"You don't have to be young to make music."

"Maybe not. But whatever muse I had back in those days pissed off and left me a long time ago. Believe me, I've tried. I used to get home from work and pick up my guitar almost every day, but the spark was just never there. I don't even try anymore."

"I hear you," I said. "I never had the genius—I just saw it in others. And when you know what you *could* be doing, when the music in your head's so far beyond what you can pull out of your instrument..."

"Why bother."

I gave a slow nod, then studied her for a moment. "So if you could go back and change something, is that what it would be? You'd go to that night and go your own way instead of hooking up with this Brian guy?"

She laughed. "I guess. Though I'd have to *apply* myself as well."

"I can send you back."

"Yeah, right."

I didn't take my gaze from those blue eyes of hers. I just repeated what I'd said. "I can send you back."

She let me hold her gaze for a couple of heartbeats, then shook her head.

"You almost had me going there," she said.

"I can send you back," I said a third time.

Third time's the charm and she looked uneasy.

"Send me back in time."

I nodded.

"To warn myself."

"No. *You'd* go back, with all you know now. And it's not really back. Time doesn't run in a straight line, it all happens at the same time. Past, present, future. It's like this is you now." I touched my left shoulder. "And this is you then." I touched the end of a finger on my left hand. "If I hold my arm straight, it seems linear, right?"

She gave me a dubious nod.

"But really —" I crooked my left arm so that my finger was touching my shoulder. " — the two times are right beside each other. It's not such a big jump."

"And you can send me there?"

I nodded. "On one condition."

"What's that?"

"You come back here on this exact same day and ask for me."

"Why?"

"Because that's how it works."

She shook her head. "This is nuts."

"Nothing to lose, everything to gain."

"I guess…"

I knew I almost had her, so I smiled and said, "Should you stay or should you go?"

Her blue gaze held mine again, then she shrugged. Picking up her beer, she chugged the last third down, then set the empty glass on the table.

"What the hell," she said. "How does it work?"

I slipped off my stool and closed the few steps between us.

"You think about that night," I said. "Think about it hard. Then I put two fingers on each of your temples — like this. And then I kiss your third eye."

I leaned forward and pressed my lips against her brow, halfway between my fingers. Held my lips there for a heartbeat. Another. Then I stepped away.

She looked at me for a long moment, before standing up. She didn't say a word, but they never do. She just laid a couple of bills on the bar to pay for her drink and walked out the door.

December 23, 2002

"I feel like I should know you," the bartender said when the girl with the dark blue hair walked into the bar and pulled up a stool.

"My name's Sarah Blue. What's yours?"

"Alphonse," he said and grinned. "And you're really Sarah Blue?" He glanced towards the doorway. "I thought you big stars only travelled with an entourage."

"All I've got is a cab waiting outside. And I'm not such a big star."

"Yeah, right. Like 'Take It to the Streets' wasn't the big hit of—when was it? Summer of '89."

"You've got a good memory."

"It was a good song."

"Yeah, it was. I never get tired of playing it. But my hit days were a long time ago. These days I'm just playing theatres and clubs again."

"Nothing wrong with that. So what can I get you?"

"Actually, I was expecting to meet a guy in here today. Do you know an Eddie Ramone?"

"Sure, I do." He shook his head. "I should have remembered."

"Remembered what?"

"Hang on."

He went to a drawer near the cash and pulled out a stack of envelopes held together with a rubber band. Flipping through them, he returned to where she was sitting and laid one out on the bar in front of her. In an unfamiliar hand was written:

Sarah Blue
December 23, 2002

"Do those all have names and dates on them?" she asked.

"Every one of them."

He showed her the top one. It was addressed to:

Jonathan Block
January 27, 2003

"You think he'll show?" she asked.

"You did."

She shook her head. "What's this all about?"

"Damned if I know. People just drop these off from time to time and sooner or later someone shows up to collect it."

"It's not just Eddie?"

"No. But most of the time it's Eddie."

"And he's not here?"

"Not today. Maybe he tells you why in the letter."

"The letter. Right."

"I'll leave you to it," Alphonse said.

He walked back to where he'd left the drawer open and dropped the envelopes in. When he looked up, she was still watching him.

"You want a drink?" he asked.

"Sure. Whatever's on tap that's dark."

"You've got it."

She returned her attention to the letter, staring at it until Alphonse returned with her beer. She thanked him, had a sip, then slid her finger into the top of the envelope and tore it open. There was a single sheet inside, written in the same unfamiliar script that was on the envelope. It said:

Hello Sarah,

Well, if you're reading this, I guess you're a believer now. I sure hope your life went where you wanted it to go this time.

Funny thing, that might amuse you. I was talking to Joe, back in the Camden Town days, and I asked him if he had any advice for a big fan who'd be devastated when he finally went to the big gig in the sky.

The first thing he said was, "Get bent."

The second was, "You really think we're ever going to make it?"

When I nodded, he thought for a moment, then said, "You tell him or her – it's a her? – tell her it's never about the player, is it? It's always about the music. And the music never dies."

And if she wanted to be a musician? I asked him.

"Tell her that whatever she takes on, stay in for the duration. Maybe you can just bang out a tune or a lyric, maybe it takes you forever. It doesn't matter how you put it together. All that matters is that it means something to you, and you play it like it means something to you. Anything else is just bollocks."

I'm thinking, if you got your life straight this time, you'd probably agree with him.

But now to business. First off, the reason I'm not here to see you is that this isn't the same future I sent you back from. That one still exists, running alongside this one, but it's closed to you because you're living that other life now. And you know there's just no point in us meeting again, because we've done what needed to be done.

At least we did it for you.

If you're in the music biz now, you know there's no such thing as a free ride. What I need you to do is, pass it on. You know how to do it. All you've got to decide is who.

Eddie

Sarah read it twice before she folded the letter up, returned it to the envelope and stowed in the pocket of her jacket. She had some more of her beer. Alphonse approached as she was setting her glass back down on the bar top.

"Did that clear it up for you?" he asked.

She shook her head.

"Well, that's Eddie for you. The original man of mystery. He ever start in on his time travel yarns with you?"

She shook her head again, but only because she wasn't ready to admit it to anyone. To do so didn't feel right, and that feeling had made her keep it to herself through all the years.

Alphonse held out his right hand. "He wanted to send me back to the day before I broke this—said I could turn my life around and live it right this time."

"And...did you?"

Alphonse laughed. "What does it look like?"

Sarah smiled. Of course, he hadn't. Not in this world. But maybe in one running parallel to it...

She thought about that night at the Standish, so long ago. The Clash playing and she was dancing, dancing, so happy, so filled with music. And she was straight, too—no drinks, no drugs that night—but high all the same. On the music. And then right in the middle of a blistering version of "Clampdown," her head just...*swelled* with this impossible lifetime that she'd never, she *couldn't* have lived.

But she knew she'd connect with a guy named Brian. And she did.

And she *knew* how it would all go downhill from there, so after the concert, when they were leaving the theatre from a side door, she blew him off. And he got pissed off and gave her a shove that knocked her down. He looked at her, sobered by what he'd done, but she waved him off. He hesitated, then walked away, and she just sat there in the alley, thinking she was going crazy. Wanting to cry.

And then someone reached a hand to her to help her up.

"You okay there?" a voice with a British accent asked.

And she was looking into Joe Strummer's face. The Joe Strummer she'd seen on stage. But superimposed over it, she saw Joe Strummers that were still to come.

The one she'd seen fronting the Pogues in...some other life.

The one she'd seen fronting the Mescaleros...

The one who'd die of a heart attack at fifty years young...

"You want me to call you a cab?" he asked.

"No. No, I'm okay. Great gig."

"Thanks."

On impulse, she gave him a kiss, then stepped back. Away. Out of his life. Into her new one.

She blinked, realizing that Alphonse was still standing by her. How long had she been spaced out?

"Well…" she said, looking for something to say. "Eddie seemed like a nice guy to me."

Alphonse nodded. "He's got a big heart—he'll give you the shirt off his back. Hasn't got much of a lip these days, but he still sits in with the band from time to time. You can't say no to a guy like that and he never tries to showboat, like he thinks he plays better than he can. He keeps it simple and puts the heart into what he's playing."

"Maybe I'll come back and catch him one night."

"Door's always open during business hours, Miss Blue."

"Sarah."

"Sarah, then. You come back any time."

He left to serve a new customer and Sarah looked around the bar. No one stood out to her—the way she assumed she had to Eddie—so she'd have to come back.

She put a couple of bills on the bar top to cover the cost of her beer and went out to look for her cab. As she got into the back seat, she found herself hoping that Eddie had made himself at least one world where he'd got his lip back. That was the only reason she could think that he kept passing along the magic of a second chance—paying back his own attempts at getting it right.

It was either that, or he was an angel.

✳

January 27, 2003

Alphonse smiled when she came in. When he started to draw her a draught, she shook her head.

"I'll have a coffee if you've got one," she said.

"We don't get much call for coffee, even at this time of day, so it's kind of grungy. Let me put on a fresh pot."

He busied himself at the coffee machine, throwing out the old grounds, inserting a filter full of new coffee.

"So what brings you in so early?" he asked when he turned back to her.

"I can't get those envelopes out of my head."

"The...oh, yeah. They're a bit of a puzzle all right. But I can't let you look at them."

"I'm not asking. But when you were giving me mine, I saw the date on the one on the top of the stack."

"Today's date," Alphonse guessed.

She nodded. "Do you mind if I hang around and wait?"

"Not at all. But it could be a long haul."

"'sokay. I've got the time."

She sat chatting with Alphonse for awhile, then retired to one of the booths near the stage with her second cup of coffee. Pulling out her journal, she did some sketches of the bar, the empty stage, Alphonse at work. The sketches were in pictures and words. At some point they might find a melody and swell into a song. Or they might not. It didn't matter to her. Doodling in her journal was just something she always did—a way to occupy time on the road and provide touchstones for her memory.

*

Jonathan Block didn't show up until that evening, after she'd had a surprisingly good Cajun stew and the band was starting to set up. He looked nothing like what she'd expected—not that she'd had any specific visual in mind. It was just that he looked like a street person. Medium height, gaunt features, a few days' worth of stubble and greasy hair, shabby clothes. She'd expected someone more...successful.

She waited until he'd collected his envelope and had a chance to read it before approaching him.

"I guess your replay didn't turn out," she said.

He gave her a look that was half wary, half confused.

"What do you mean?" he asked.

She pulled out her own envelope, creased and wrinkled from living in her pocket for over a month, and showed it to him.

"Do you feel like talking?" she asked. "I'll buy you a drink."

He hesitated, then shrugged. "Sure. I'll have a ginger ale."

She got one for him from Alphonse, then led Jonathan back to her booth.

"What did you want to talk about?" he asked.

"You have to ask? I mean, this, all of this…" She laid her envelope on the Formica table top between them. "It's just so strange."

He gave a slow nod and laid his own down beside his drink.

"But it's real, isn't it?" he said. "The letters prove that."

"What happened to you? Why didn't it work out?"

"What makes you think it didn't?"

"I'm sorry. It's just…the way you…you know…"

"No, I should be the one apologizing. It was a fair question." He looked past her for a moment, then returned his gaze to hers. "It worked for me and it didn't. I just didn't think it through carefully enough. I should have focused on a point in time *before* I got drunk—before I even had a problem with drinking. But I didn't. So when I went back the three years, suddenly I'm in the car again, pissed out of my mind, and I know that the other car's going to come around the corner, and I know I'm going to hit it, and I know it's too late to just pull over."

He wasn't telling her much, but Sarah was able to fill in the details for herself.

"Oh, how horrible," she said.

"Yeah, it wasn't very bright on my part. But hey, who'd have ever thought that a thing like that would even work? When he kissed me on my forehead I thought he was just some freaky guy getting some weird little thrill. I was going to take a swing at him, but then I was there. Back in the car. On that night."

"What happened?"

"Well, the good thing was, even drunk as I was, I knew what was coming and whatever else I might have been, I wasn't a bad guy. Thoughtless as shit, oh yeah, but not bad. So instead of letting myself hit the car, I just drove into a lamppost in the couple of moments I had left. The twelve-year-old girl who would have died — who *did* die the first time around — was spared."

"And you?"

"Serious injuries. I didn't have any medical, so I lost everything paying for the bills. Lost my job. Got charged with drunk driving, and it wasn't the first time, but since I hadn't hurt anybody, they just took away my license. But after that it was pretty much the same slide downhill that it was the first time."

"You don't sound…" Sarah wasn't sure how to put it.

"Much broke up about it?"

"Yeah, I guess."

"It's like I told you," he said. "This time the little girl lived. I wasn't any less stupid, but this time no one else had to pay for my stupidity. I've still got a chance to put my life back together. I've been sober since that night. I just need a break, a chance to get cleaned up and back on my feet. I know I can do it."

Sarah nodded. Then she asked the question that troubled her the most.

"Did you ever try to change anything else?" she asked.

"What do you mean?"

"Some disaster where a little forewarning could save a lot of lives."

"You mean like 9/11?"

"Yeah. Or the bombing in Oklahoma."

He shook his head. "It's a funny thing. As soon as I heard about them, it all came back, that I'd been around when they happened the first time and I *remembered*. But the memory just wasn't there until it actually happened."

"Like all we're changing is our own lives."

"Pretty much. And even that's walking blind, the further you get from familiar territory."

Sarah knew exactly what he meant. It had been easy to change things at first, but once she was in a life that was so different from how it had gone the first time, there were no more touchstones and you had to do like everybody did: do what you could and hope for the best.

"I was afraid there was something wrong with me," she said. "That I was so self-centered that I just couldn't be bothered with anything that didn't personally touch my life."

"You don't really believe that."

"How would you know?"

"Well, c'mon. You're Sarah Blue. You're like a poster child for causes."

"I never told you my name."

He smiled and shook his head. "What? Suddenly you're anonymous? Maybe the charts got taken over by all these kids with their bare midriffs, but there was a time not so long ago when you were always on the cover of some magazine or other."

She shrugged, not knowing what to say.

"I don't know what your life was like the first time around," he went on, "but you've been making a difference this time out. So don't be so hard on yourself."

"I guess."

They sat quietly for a moment. Sarah looked around the bar and saw that the clientele had changed. The afternoon boozehounds had given way to a younger, hipper crowd, though she could still spot a few grey heads in the crowd. These were the people who'd come for the music, she realized.

"Will you do like it says in the letter?" she asked, turning back to her companion.

"You mean pass it on?"

She nodded.

"First chance I get."

"Me, too," she said. "And I think my go at it should be to help you."

"You haven't passed it on yet?"

She shook her head.

"I don't know if you get a third try," he said.

She shrugged. "If it doesn't work out, I can always front you some money, give you a chance to get back on your feet, and use the whatever-the-hell-it-is on someone else."

"You'd do that for me — just like that?"

"Wouldn't you?"

He gave a slow nod. "Not before. But now, yeah. In a heartbeat." He looked at her for a long moment. "How'd you know I'd be here?"

"I saw your name and the date on your envelope when I was collecting my own. I just…needed to talk to someone about it and Eddie doesn't seem to be available."

"Eddie," he said. "What do you think he is?"

"An angel."

"So you believe in God?"

"I…I'm not sure. But I believe in good and evil. I guess I just naturally think of somebody working on the side of good as being an angel."

He nodded. "It's as good a description as any."

"So let's give this a shot," she said. "Only this time —"

"Concentrate on a point in time where I can made the decision not to drink before it's too late."

She nodded.

She gave him a moment, turning her attention back to the bandstand. Looks like tonight they had a keyboard player, a guitarist, a bass player, a drummer, and a guy on saxophones. They were still tuning, adjusting the drum kit, soaking the reeds for the saxes.

She turned back to Jonathan.

"Have you got it?" she asked.

"Yeah. I think I do."

"I'm not going to try to tell you how to live your life, but I think it helps to have something bigger than yourself to believe in."

"Like God?"

She shrugged.

"Or like a cause?" he added.

She smiled. "Like a whatever. Are you ready?"

"Do it," he said. "And thanks."

She leaned over the table, put her hands on his temples and kissed him where Eddie had kissed her, on—what had he called it? Her third eye. She kept her lips pressed against his forehead for a couple of moments, then sat back in her seat.

"Don't forget to come back here on the same day," she said.

But Jonathan only gave her a puzzled look. Without speaking, he got up and left the booth. Sarah tracked him as he made his way through the growing crowd, but he never once looked back.

Weird. How was she even supposed to know if it had worked? But she guessed that in this world, she wouldn't.

Her gaze went to Jonathan's half-drunk ginger ale and she noticed that he'd left his letter behind. There was another puzzle. How did they go from world to world, future to future?

Maybe it had something to do with the Rhatigan itself. Maybe there was something about the bar that made it a crossroads for all these futures.

She thought of asking Alphonse, but got the sense that he didn't know. Or if he knew, he wouldn't be telling. But maybe if she could track down Eddie...

He appeared beside her table as though her thoughts had summoned him.

"Never thought about third chances," he said.

He slid a trumpet case onto the booth seat, then sat down beside it, smiling at her from the other side of the table.

"Is—was that against the rules?" she asked.

He shrugged. "What rules? The only thing that's important is for you to come back and get the message to pass it on."

"But what *is* it that we're passing on? Where did this thing come from?"

"Sometimes it's better to just accept that something is, instead of trying to take it apart."

"But—"

"Because when you take it apart, it might not work any more. You wouldn't want that, would you, Sarah?"

"No. Of course not. But I've got so many questions..."

He made a motion with his hands like he was breaking something, then he held out his palms looking down at them with a sad expression.

"Okay, I get the point already," she said. "But you've got to understand my curiosity."

"Sure, I do. And all I'm doing is asking you to let it go."

"But...can you at least tell me who you are?"

"Eddie Ramone."

"And he's...?"

"Just a guy who's learned how to give a few people the tools to fix a mistake they might have made. Doesn't work on everybody, and not everybody gets it right when they do go back. But I give them another shot. Think of me as a messenger of hope."

Sarah felt as though she was going to burst with the questions that were swelling inside her.

"So'd you bring a guitar?" Eddie asked.

She blinked, then shook her head. "No. But I don't play jazz."

"Take a cue from Norah Jones. Anything can swing, even a song by Hank Williams...or Sarah Blue."

She shook her head. "These people didn't come to hear me."

"No, they came to hear music. They don't give a rat's ass who's playing it, just so long as it's real."

"Okay. Maybe." But then she had a thought. "Just answer this one thing for me."

He smiled, waiting.

"In your letter you said that this is a different time line from the one I first met you in."

"That's right, it is."

"So how come you're here and you know me in this one?"

"Something's got to be the connection," he told her.

"But—"

He opened his case and took out his trumpet. Getting up, he reached for her hand.

"C'mon. Jackie'll lend you his guitar for a couple of numbers. All you've got to do is tell us the key."

She gave up and let him lead her to where the other musicians were standing at the side of the stage.

"Oh, and don't forget," Eddie said as they were almost there. "Before you leave the bar, you need to write your own letter to Jonathan."

"I feel like I'm going crazy."

"'Crazy,'" Eddie said. "Willie Nelson. That'd make a nice start — you know, something everybody knows."

Sarah wanted to bring the conversation back to where she felt she needed it to go, but a look into his eyes gave her a sudden glimpse of a hundred thousand different futures, all banging up against each other in a complex, twisting pattern that gave her a touch of vertigo. So she took a breath instead, shook her head and just let him introduce her to the other musicians.

Jackie's Gibson semi-hollow body was a lot like one of her own guitars — it just had a different pickup. She took a seat on the center-stage stool and adjusted the height of the microphone, then started playing the opening chords of "Tony Adams." It took her a moment to find the groove she was looking for, that hip-hop swing that Strummer and the Mescaleros had given the song. By the time she found it, the piano and bass had come in, locking them into the groove.

She glanced at Eddie. He stood on the side of the stage, holding his horn, swaying gently to the rhythm. Smiling, she turned back to the mike and started to sing the first verse.

For Joe Strummer, R.I.P.

The Butter Spirit's Tithe

I

It happened just as we were finishing our first set at the Hole in Tucson, Arizona, running through a blistering version of "The Bucks of Oranmore" — one of the *big* box tunes, so far as I'm concerned. Miki was bouncing so much in her seat that I thought her accordion was going to fly off her knee. I had a cramp in the thumb of my pick hand, but I was damned if that'd stop me from seeing the piece through to the end, no matter how fast she played it.

So of course she picked up the speed again, grinning at me as we kicked into our third run through the tune. I grinned back, adding a flourish of jazzy chords that I shouldn't have had the space to fit in, but I managed all the same. It's the kind of thing that happens when you play live and was nothing I'd be able to duplicate again. Miki raised an eyebrow, suitably impressed.

And then, just as we came up on a big finish, all the strings on my guitar broke, even the bass "E." I snapped my head back, which probably saved me from losing an eye, but I got a couple of wicked cuts on my chording hand.

Needless to say, that brought the tune to a ragged finish. Miki stared at me for a long moment, then turned back to her mike.

"We're taking a short break," she said, "while Conn restrings his guitar. Don't go away and remember to tip your waitress."

I reached over to the P.A.'s board and shut off the sound from the stage, switching the house speakers back to the mix of country and Tex-Mex that the bar got from some satellite feed. Then I sucked at the cuts on my hand. Miki dropped the strap from her accordion and set the instrument on the floor.

"Jesus, Mary, and Joseph," she said, sounding more like her brother than I'd ever tell her. "What the hell just happened?"

I shrugged. "Guess I got a set of bum strings. It happens."

"Yeah, right. Every string breaking at the same time." She paused and studied me for a moment. "Has it happened before?"

I shook my head. I was telling the truth. But other things just as strange had — no more than two or three times a year, but that was two or three times too many.

I set my guitar in its stand and went to the back of the stage where I got my string-winder and a fresh set of strings. Miki was still sitting on her stool when I got back to my own seat. Usually she'd be off the stage by now, mixing with the audience.

"So what aren't you telling me?" she asked.

"What makes you think I'm not telling you something?"

"You've got that look on your face."

"What look?"

"Your 'holding back something juicy' look."

"Well, it *was* strange to have them all break at once like that."

"Try impossible," she said.

"You saw it."

"Yeah, and I still don't quite believe it. So give."

I shook my head.

"It's nothing you want to hear," I told her.

She stood and came over to my side of the stage so that I had to look up at her. Though perhaps "up" was stretching it some since she wasn't much taller than me, and I was still sitting down. Her hair was bright orange this week, short and messy as ever, but it suited her. Truth is, there isn't much that doesn't suit her. She might be too small and compact to ever be hired to walk down the runway at a fashion show, but she could wear anything and make it look better than it ever would on a professional model.

Tonight she was in baggy green cargos and a black Elvis Costello T-shirt that she'd cut the arms off of, but she still looked like a million dollars. She'd kill me if I ever said this in her hearing—because she's probably the best button accordion player I've ever heard; certainly the best I've ever played with—but I'm sure that half the reason we sell out most of our shows is because of her looks. Sort of pixie gamine meets sexy punk. It drew the young crowd, but she was too cute to put off the older listeners. And like I said, she can *play*.

"I just asked, didn't I?" she said.

"Yeah, but…"

I'd learned not to talk about certain things around her because it just set her off. I can still remember asking her if she ever read any Yeats—this was in the first week we were out on the road as a duo. She'd given up on fronting a band, because it cost too much to keep the four-piece on the road, and had hired me to be her accompanist in their place.

"Don't get me started on Yeats," she'd said.

"What's wrong with Yeats?"

"Yeats, personally? Nothing, so far as I know. I never met the man. And I'll admit he had a way with the words. What I don't like about him is all that Celtic Twilight shite he was always on about."

I shook my head.

"What?" she said.

I shrugged. "I don't know. It just seems that for a woman born in Ireland, who makes her living play-ing Celtic music, you don't care much for your own traditions."

"What traditions? I like a good Guinness and play the dance tunes on my box—those are traditions I can appreciate. I can even enjoy a good game of foot-ball, if I'm in the mood, which isn't bloody often. What I don't like is when people get into all that mystical shite." She laughed, but without a lot of humour. "And I don't know which is worse, the wannabe Celts or those who think they were born to pass on the great Secret Traditions."

"Which is a good portion of your audience — especially on the concert circuit."

She had a sip of her draught and smiled at me over the brim of her glass. "Well, you know what they say. Doesn't matter what your line of work, there'll always be punters."

This was so Miki, I soon discovered. She was either irrepressibly cheerful and ready to joke about anything, or darkly cynical about the world at large, and the Irish in particular. But she hadn't always been this way.

I didn't know her well before she hired me, but we'd been at a lot of the same sessions and ran with the same crowd, so I already had more than a passing acquaintance with the inimitable Ms. Greer before we started touring together.

Time was she was the definition of good-natured, so much so that a conversation with her could give some people a toothache. It was her brother Donal who was the morose one. But something happened to Donal — I never quite got all the details. I just know he died hard. Overseas, I think. In the Middle East or some place like that. Some desert, anyway. Whatever had happened, Miki took it badly and she hadn't been the same since. Now she was either up or she was down and even her good humour could often have a dark undercurrent to it. Not so much mean, as bitter.

None of which explained her dislike of things Irish, particularly the more mystical side of the Celtic tradition. I could understand her distancing herself from her roots — I might, too, if I'd been brought up the way she had by a drunken father, eventually living on the streets with Donal, the two of them barely in their teens. But while my background's Irish, I grew up in the Green, what they used to call the Irish section of Tyson before it got taken over, first by the bohemians, and then more recently by the new waves of immigrants from countries whose names I can barely pronounce.

The families living in the Green were dirt-poor — some of us still didn't have hot water and electricity in the fifties — but we looked after each other. There was a sense of community in the Green that Miki never got to experience. I'm not saying everyone was an angel. Our fathers worked long hours and drank hard. There were fights in and outside of the bars every night. But if you lost your job, your neighbours would step in and see you through. No one had to go on relief. And my dad, at least, never took out his hardships on his family the way Miki's did.

There was magic in the Green, too. It lay waiting for you in the stories told around the kitchen stoves, in the songs sung in the parlors. I grew up on great heaps of Miki's "Celtic Twilight shite," except it was less airy, more down-to-earth. Stories of leprechauns and banshees and strange black dogs that followed a man home.

And, at least according to my dad, not all of it was just stories.

"Well?" Miki said.

"Well, what?"

"Do you need a bang on the ear to get you going?"

"It's a long story," I said.

She looked at her watch. "Then you better get started, because we're back on in twenty minutes."

I sighed. But as I restrung my guitar, I told her about it.

2

I remember my dad took me aside the day I was leaving home. We stood on the stoop outside our tenement building, hands in our pockets, looking down the street to the traffic going by at the far end of the block, across the way to where the Cassidy girls were playing hopscotch, anywhere but at each other.

"If it was just a need for work, Conn," he finally said, trying one more time to understand. "But this talk of having to find yourself…"

How to explain? With four sisters and three brothers, I felt smothered. Especially since each and every one of them knew exactly what they wanted out of life. They had it all mapped out — the jobs, the marriages, the children, the life here in the Green. There were no unknown territories for them.

I only had the music, and while it was respected in our family, it wasn't considered a career option. It was what we did in the evenings, around our kitchen table and those of our neighbours.

I'd tried to put it into words before today, but it always came out sounding like I was turning my back on them, and that wasn't the case. I just needed to find a place in the world that I could make my own. A way to make a living without the help of an uncle or a cousin. It might not be music. But with a limited education, and the even more limited interest in furthering what I did have, music seemed the best option I had.

Besides, I lived and breathed music.

"I know you don't understand," I said. "But it's what I need to do. I'm only going to Newford and I won't be gone forever."

"But wouldn't it be easier on you to live with us while you...while you try this?"

I'll give them this: my parents didn't understand, but they were supportive, nevertheless.

I shook my head. "I need the space, dad. And there aren't the venues here like there are in the city."

He gave a slow nod. And maybe he even understood.

"When you do find yourself a place," he said, "make peace with its spirits."

I guess you might find that an odd thing for him to say, but we O'Neills are a superstitious lot. "Everything has a spirit," dad would tell us when we were growing up. "So give everything its proper respect or you'll be bringing the bad luck down upon yourself."

The presence of spirits wasn't something we talked about a lot — and certainly not in the mystical way people do now, where it's all about communicating with energy patterns through crystals, candles, or whatever. It was just accepted that the spirits were here, all around us, sharing the world with us: Ghosts and sheerie. Merrow, skeaghshee and butter spirits. All kinds.

"I will," I told him.

He pressed a folded twenty into my hand — a lot of money for us in those days — then embraced me in a powerful hug. I'd already said my other goodbyes inside.

"There'll always be room for you here," he said.

I nodded, my throat suddenly too thick to speak. I'd wanted and planned for this for months and suddenly I was tottering on the edge of giving it all up and going to work at the factory with my brothers. But I hoisted my duffel bag in one hand, my home-made guitar case in the other. It was made of scavenged plywood and weighed more than the instrument did.

"Thanks, dad," I said. "Just…thanks."

We both knew that simple word encompassed far more than the twenty dollars he'd just given me and the reminder that I'd always have a home to return to.

He clapped me on the shoulder and then I turned and headed down the street where I had an appointment with a Newford-bound bus.

*

Things didn't go as planned.

I'd set up a few gigs before I left home, but my act didn't go over all that well. I'm not a strong singer, so I need the audience to actually be listening to me for them to appreciate the songs. But people don't have that kind of patience in a bar. Or maybe it's simply a lack of interest. They've gone out to drink and have fun with their friends and the music's only supposed to be background.

"You're a brilliant guitarist," the owner of the bar I played on the second weekend told me. "But it's wasted on this lot. You should hook up with a fiddler, or somebody with a bigger presence. You know, something to grab their attention and hold it."

In other words, I wasn't much of a front person. As though to punctuate the point, he didn't book me for another gig.

Worse, I knew he was right. I didn't like being up there on those little stages by myself and even though I knew nobody was really listening, I could barely mumble my way through my introductions. It was different sitting around the kitchen at home, or in a session. I loved backing up the fiddlers and pipers, the flute and box players. And when I did sing a song, people listened.

So I put the word out that I was available as an accompanist, but all the decent players already had their own and the people who did contact me weren't much good. It was so frustrating. I ended up taking gigs with some of them anyway, but they didn't challenge me musically or help my bank balance — my bank being the left front pocket of my cargo pants which I could at least button closed.

I ended up busking a lot — in the market, at subway entrances, down by Fitzhenry Park — but since I didn't have enough presence on stage where I had the benefit of a sound system, I sure didn't have what it took to grab the attention of passersby on the street, where I was competing with all the traffic and city noise as well as audience indifference. My take after playing was never more than a few dollars. By the end of a month I was out of money and had to leave the boarding house where I was staying. I ended up in Squatland, sleeping in one of the many abandoned buildings there with the other homeless people, keeping my busking money for food.

I could have gone home, I guess. But I was too proud. Though not too proud to find another way to make a living.

I finally found a job as a janitor at the Sovereign Building on Flood Street. I got the gig through Joey Bennett, this cab driver I met when I was busking at the gates of Fitzhenry Park. He'd stand outside his cab, arms folded across his chest, listening to me while he waited for a fare. He was a jazz buff, but we got to talking on my breaks. When he heard I was looking for work, it turned out he knew a lawyer who had an office in the Sovereign and the lawyer got me the job.

I guess it wasn't much different than getting a job through an uncle or cousin, except Joey and the lawyer were my connections. I'd done this on my own.

I didn't mind the job that much. I like seeing things put to order and kept clean, and it's very meditative being in a big building like that, pretty much on my own. There are other cleaners, but we each have our own floors and we don't really see each other except at break time.

Now here's the thing.

I'd paid my respects to the spirits at the boarding house, and later my squat—feeling a little foolish while I talked into thin air to do so. No one answered and I didn't expect them to. But I never thought about doing it at work. So, when I saw the kid tracking muddy footprints down the hall I'd just spent a half hour mopping down, I wasn't thinking of house spirits and respect. I just told him off.

When he turned in my direction, I saw that he wasn't really a kid—more a kid-sized, little man with brown skin and hair that looked like Rasta dreadlocks. He was wearing a dark green cap and shirt, brown-green trousers and was barefoot—unless you counted the mud on them as footwear. Over his shoulder, he had a coil of rope with a grappling hook fastened to one end. In his hand, he carried a small cloth bag that bulged with whatever it was holding.

It was raining outside, so it wasn't hard to figure out where the mud had come from. How he'd gotten *into* the building was a whole other story. Used the grappling hook to get up the side of the wall, I suppose, and then forced a window.

He glared at me when I yelled at him, dark eyes flashing.

"How'd you get in here, anyway?" I demanded.

He pointed a gnarled finger at me.

"I give you seven years," he said in this gravelly voice that felt like it should have come from a much larger person.

"Yeah, well, I'll give you thirty seconds to get out of here," I told him.

"Do you know who I am?"

Until he said that, I hadn't actually considered it. Not after my first impression when I thought he was just some kid, nor when I realized that he was this weird little man who'd somehow found his way into this locked office building. But as soon as he asked, I knew. And my heart sank. I'd done the very thing my dad had always warned us against.

Though I'll tell you, while I grew up with his stories of fairies and such, accepting them the way you do things that are spoken of in your family, I'd never really believed in them. It was like any other superstition—spilling salt, walking under ladders, that kind of thing. Most people don't believe, but they avoid such situations all the same, just in case. Which is why I'd paid my respects to invisible presences in the boarding house and my squat. Just in case.

"Listen," I began, "I didn't realize who—"

But he cut me off.

"Seven years," he repeated.

"Seven years and what?"

"You'll be my tithe to the Grey Man."

My dad had stories about this as well. How the brolaghan known as Old Boneless was like a Mafia don to the smaller fairies, offering them his protection in return for a tithe—the main protection he offered being that he himself wouldn't hurt them. The tithe could be anything from tasty morsels, beer or whiskey, to pilfered knickknacks and even changelings. It just had to be something stolen from the human world.

Dad's stories didn't say what the Grey Man did with any of these things. Being a creature of mist and fog, you wouldn't think he'd have any use for material items. Maybe they helped make him more substantial.

I certainly didn't want to find out firsthand.

"Wait a sec'," I said. "All I did was—"

"Disrespect me. And just to remind you of my displeasure," he added.

He pointed that gnarled finger at me again and my pants came undone, falling down around my ankles. By the time I'd stooped to pull them up, he was gone. I zipped up my fly and redid my belt.

They came undone and my pants fell down once more.

I suppose that's what really convinced me that I'd just had an encounter with a genuine fairy man. No matter how often I tried, I couldn't get my pants to stay up. Finally, I sat down there in the hall holding them in place with one hand while I tried to figure out what to do.

Nothing came to mind.

And the worst thing about it, there was this totally cute girl named Nita Singh that I'd been spending my breaks with. She worked the floor below mine and while I hadn't quite figured out yet if she was seeing anybody, she was friendly enough to give me hope that maybe she wasn't. She certainly seemed to return my interest.

So of course she had to come up looking for me when I didn't come down at break time.

"Are you okay?" she asked as she came down the hall from the stairwell.

Nita was almost as tall as me, with shoulder-length, straight dark brown hair tied back in a pony-tail. Like all of us, she was wearing grubby jeans and a T-shirt, but they looked much better on her.

"Oh sure," I said. "I'm just…you know, having a rest."

She leaned her back against the wall, then slid down until she was sitting beside me. She glanced at how I was holding my jeans and grinned.

"Having some trouble with your pants?"

I shrugged. "I think my zipper's broken."

From the first night I'd met her, all I'd ever wanted was to be close to her. Now I just wanted her to go away.

"Maybe I can fix it," she said.

In any other circumstance, could this have played out any better?

"I don't think so," I told her.

I couldn't believe I had to say that. She was going to think I was such a dork, but instead she gave me a knowing look.

"Had a run-in with the local butter spirit, did you?" she asked.

Butter spirits were supposed to be a kind of house fairy related to leprechauns, but much more thieving and malicious. Back home they especially enjoyed fresh butter and would draw the "good" of the milk before it was churned.

I blinked in surprise. "How do you know about that kind of thing?"

"Daddy-ji's Indian," she said, "but my mum's Irish. There was a big to-do when they hooked up. You know, son disowned, the whole bit."

"I'm sorry."

She shrugged. "Not your fault. Anyway, mum was forever telling stories about the little people."

"My dad did, too."

"I just never thought they were more than stories."

"But you do now? Have you seen him?"

She nodded. "Not up close. But I've caught glimpses of him and his little grappling hook that he uses to clamber up the outside walls. I think he pilfers food and drink from the bars and restaurants in Chinatown. I've seen him leave empty-handed, but return with a bag full of something or other."

"You never said anything before."

"What was I going to say? I thought you'd be telling me about him soon enough. And if you didn't, what would you think of me, telling you stories like that?"

"Has anyone else seen him?"

She laughed. "How do you think you got this job?"

"I don't understand."

"I've been working here for almost nine months and you've lasted the longest of anybody who's worked this floor in all that time. How long have you been here?"

"Almost a month."

"Most people don't last a week. There's almost always an opening for the job on this floor. Management tries to shift some of us to it, but we just threaten to quit when they do."

"So that's why it was so dirty when I first came on."

She nodded.

"And it's the butter spirit that scares people off?"

"Most people just think this floor is haunted, but you and I know better."

"They got on the wrong side of him," I said. "Like I just did."

"Don't worry," she told me. "Whatever he's done—"

"Fixed it so my pants won't stay up."

She grinned. "It doesn't last."

"Well, I can work in my boxers, but I don't know how I'm going to get home."

"If it's not gone by then, we'll see if we can rustle up a long coat for you to wear."

3

"So I'm assuming it wore off," Miki said when I was done.

I nodded. "Before I left the building at the end of my shift."

"Then what was tonight all about?"

"He likes to remind me that the tithe is still coming due."

Miki got a hard look. "You see what I mean about how this is all shite?"

She looked off the stage, trying to see if the little bogle man was in view, I assumed. He wasn't. Or at least he wasn't visible. I knew, because I'd already checked.

"It's not shite," I said. "It's real."

"I know. It's shite because it does no one any good. There's a reason the Queen of the Fairies gave Yeats that warning."

"What warning?"

"He was seeing this medium and through her, the Fairy Queen told him, 'Be careful, and do not seek to know too much about us.' But do any of the punters listen?"

"I wasn't trying to find out anything about them."

She nodded. "I got that. My point is, any contact with them is a sure recipe for heartache and trouble."

She had that much right.

"You don't seem any more surprised by this than Nita was," I said.

"I'm not. Messing about with shite like this is what got Donal killed."

"I didn't know."

"Well, it's not something I'm going to shout out to the world." She paused a moment, then added, "So what happened with Nita? She sounded nice from what you had to say about her."

"She's wonderful. But that little bugger made her allergic to me and *that* spell hasn't worn off yet. Whenever she gets physically near to me, her nose starts running and she breaks out in hives. Sometimes her throat just closes down and she can't breathe."

I finished tightening my last string, dropped the string-winder under my stool, and plugged my guitar into my electronic tuner.

"We seem to still be able to talk on the phone," I added.

"Is that who you're always calling?"

I nodded. I didn't have a better friend in the world than Nita. And at one time, we'd been far more than that. But the butter spirit thought making her allergic to me would be a good joke—especially when he didn't let the enchantment wear off. Talking on the phone was all we had now.

"I always thought it was one of your brothers or sisters," Miki said.

"Nita's *like* a sister now," I told her, unable to keep the hurt from my voice.

Miki gave me a sympathetic look.

"So it's not just breaking guitar strings and pulling your pants down," she said.

"Christ, that's the least of it. Mostly things happen in private. Shutting off the hot water on me when I'm having a shower. Or fixing it so that the electricity doesn't work—but only in the room where I am. It's the big jokes that I dread. Once I was in a coffee shop and he curdled all the dairy products just as I was halfway through a latte. There were people puking on the tables that day and I was one of them."

Miki grimaced.

"And then there was the time I was downtown and he vanished all the stitches and buttons in what I was wearing. It's the middle of a snowstorm, and suddenly I'm standing there trying to cover myself with all these pieces of cloth that once were clothes."

"And you've never said anything about it."

I gave her a humourless smile. "Well, it's not something I want to shout out to the world either."

"Good point," she said. She paused for a moment, then added, "We're just going to have to find a way to turn the little bugger off."

I didn't want to feel the hope that rose at her words, but I couldn't help it.

"Do you know a way to do it?" I asked.

She shook her head and my frail surge of hope fled. But this was Miki. Determined, tough.

"Only that doesn't mean we can't find out," she said. "You wouldn't know this butter spirit's name, would you?"

I shook my head.

"Too bad, but I suppose that would have been too easy."

"What use would his name be?"

"There's power in names," she said. "Don't you pay attention to the stories? Just because it's all shite doesn't mean it isn't true."

"Right."

I was having trouble relating to this conversation. I mean, to be having it with Miki, of all people. Who knew that behind her disdain, she was such an expert?

"When's the tithe due?" she asked.

"April thirtieth."

She gave a slow nod. "Cally Berry's night."

"You've lost me."

"They call her the Old Woman of Gloominess. She's the blue-skinned daughter of the sun and rules the world between Halloween and Beltane. On the last day of April she throws her ruling staff away and turns into stone for the next half of the year — why do you think there are so many stone goddess images louting about in Ireland? But on that night, when she gives up her rule to the Summer Goddess, the fairies run free—like they do on Halloween. Babies are stolen and changelings left in their cribs. Debts and tithes are paid."

"Lovely."

"Mmm. I wonder if we have a gig that night..."

She took out her Palm Pilot and looked up our schedule.

"Of course we do," she said. "We're in Harnett's Point at the Harp & Tankard, from the Wednesday through Saturday. Close enough to Newford for trouble, though I guess distance doesn't seem to be a problem with him, does it?"

I shook my head. We were halfway across the country in Arizona at the moment and that hadn't stopped him.

"Actually, that can work to our advantage," she went on. "I know some people living close to Harnett's Point who might be able to help. We'll put together some smudgesticks...let's see...rosemary, rue, blackthorn, and hemlock. That'll be pungent to burn indoors, but it'll keep him off you."

"You really think you can stop him?" I asked. "I mean, it's not just the butter spirit. There's the Grey Man, too."

She nodded. "Old Boneless. Another of those damned hard men that we Irish seem to be so good at conjuring up, both in our fairies and ourselves. But I have a special fondness for the bashing of hard men, Conn, you'll see. Now tell me, how intimate were you and Nita?"

"Jeez, that's hardly —"

She held up a hand before I could finish. "I'm not prying. I just need to know if you have a bond of flesh or just words."

"We were…very intimate. Until he pulled this allergy business."

She gave me another one of her thoughtful nods.

"What are you thinking?" I asked.

"Nothing. Not yet. I'm just putting together the pieces in my head. Setting them up against what I know and what I have to find out."

"Not that I'm ungrateful," I said, "but you seem awfully familiar with this kind of thing for someone so dead set against it."

She grin she gave me was empty of humour. It was a wolf's grin. Feral.

"It's the first rule of war," she told me. "Know your enemy."

War, I thought. When did this become a war? But maybe for her it was. Maybe it should be that way for me.

"So what's Nita doing these days?" Miki asked.

"She's a social worker. She was working on her degree when I met her at the Sovereign Building."

"Is she with the city?"

I nodded.

"And you still love her? She still loves you?"

"Well, we're not celibate — I mean, it's been six and a half years now. We had six months together before the butter spirit conjured up this allergy, but…" I shrugged. "So, yes, we still love each other, but we see other people." I paused, then added, "And you need to know this because?"

"I need to know everything I can about the situation. You do want me to help, don't you?"

"I'll take any help I can get."

"Good man. So, are you all tuned up yet?" she asked, abruptly shifting conversational gears. When I nodded, she added, "Then I think it's time to start playing again."

I was going to have to fight the tuning of my guitar for the rest of the night as this new set of strings settled. But better that — better to lose myself in the mechanics of playing and tuning and the spirit of the music — than to have to think about that damned butter spirit for the next hour or so.

Except I never did get him out of my head. At the very least, throughout the set, I carried the worry of my strings snapping on me again.

4

Miki wasn't at all forthcoming about her plan to deal with the butter spirit. The first time I pressed her harder for details — "Hello," I told her. "This concerns me, you know." — she just said something about the walls having ears and if she spoke her plan aloud, she might as well write it out and hand it over the enemy.

"Trust me, Conn," she said.

So I did. She might get broody. She might carry a hard, dark anger around inside her. But it was never directed at me and I knew I could trust her with my life. Which was a good thing because if the Grey Man ever did get hold of me, it was my life that was forfeit.

*

The month went by quickly.

We finished up our gigs in the Southwest, did a week that took us up through Berkeley and Portland, and then we were back in Newford and it was time to start the two-hour drive out to Harnett's Point for our opening night at the Harp & Tankard.

Harnett's Point used to be a real backwoods village, its population evenly divided between the remnant of back-to-the-earth hippies who tended organic farms west of the city and locals who made their living off of the tourists that swelled the village in the summer. But it had changed in the last decade, becoming, like so many of the other small villages around Newford, a satellite community for those who could afford the ever pricier real estate and didn't mind the two-hour commute to their jobs.

And where once it had only the one Irish bar — Murphy's, a log and plaster-covered concrete affair near the water that was a real roadhouse — now it sported a half-dozen, including the Tankard & Horn where we were playing tonight.

Have you ever noticed how there seems to be an Irish pub on almost every corner these days? They're as bad as coffee shops. I can remember a time when the only place you could get a decent Guinness was in Ireland, and as for the music, forget it. "Traditional music" was all that Irish-American twaddle popularized by groups like the Irish Rovers. Some of them were lovely songs, once, but they'd been reduced to noisy bar jokes by the time I got into the music professionally. And then there were the folks who'd demand "some real Irish songs" like "The Unicorn," and would get all affronted when first, you wouldn't play it for them, and second, you told them it was actually written by Shel Silverstein, the same Jewish songwriter responsible for hits like Dr. Hook & the Medicine Show's "Cover of the Rolling Stone."

Miki and I played an even mix of bars, small theatres, colleges, and festivals, and I usually liked the bars the least — probably a holdover from when I was first trying to get into the music in a professional capacity. But Miki loved them. It made no sense to me why she kept taking these bookings — she could easily fill any medium-sized hall — but they kept her honest, she liked to say. "And besides," she'd add, "music and the drink, they just go together."

When we got to the Tankard & Horn that afternoon we were met out back where we parked our van by a Native American fellow. Miki introduced him to me as Tommy. I thought he was with the bar — after all, he helped us bring in our gear and set up, then settled behind the soundboard while we did our soundcheck — but he turned out to be a friend of hers and in on her secret plan. After we got the sound right, he lit a pair of smudgesticks and then he and Miki waved them around the stage until the area reeked. They weren't sweetgrass or sage, but made of the herbs and twigs that Miki had told me about back at the Hole: rosemary and rue, blackthorn and hemlock.

The smell lingered long after they were done — which was the whole point, I suppose — and didn't make it particularly pleasant to be up here in it. I wasn't the only one to feel that way. I noticed as the audience started to take their seats that people would come up to the front tables, then retreat to ones further back after a few moments. It was only when the back of the room was full that the closer tables filled up.

The audience was part yuppies, part the local holdover hippies, with a few of the long-time residents of the area standing in the back by the bar. You could tell them by their plaid flannel shirts and baseball caps. There were also a number of older Native women scattered throughout the room and I wondered why they didn't sit together. I could tell that they knew each other — or at least they all knew Tommy, since before he got back to the soundboard, he made a point of stopping and chatting with each of them.

"Do you know the song 'Tam Lin?'" Miki asked.

Tommy was back on the board now and we were getting ready to start the first set.

"Sure. It's in A minor, right?"

"Not the tune—the ballad."

I shook my head. "I know it to hear it, but I've never actually sat down and learned it."

"Still you know the story."

"Yeah. Why—"

"Keep it in mind for later," she told me.

Her mysteriousness was beginning to get on my nerves. No, that wasn't entirely fair. What had me on edge was the knowledge that tonight was the night the butter spirit meant to make me his tithe to Old Boneless.

"Don't forget now," she said.

"I won't."

Though what "Tam Lin" had to do with anything, I had no idea. I tried to remember the story as I checked my foot pedals and finished tuning my guitar. It involved a love triangle between the knight Tam Lin, the Queen of the Fairies and a mortal woman named Janet, or sometimes Jennet. Janet loved Tam Lin and he loved her, but the Fairy Queen stole him away and took him back with her to Fairyland. To win him back, Janet had to pull him down from his horse during a fairy rade on Halloween and then hold onto him while the Fairy Queen turned him into all sorts of different kinds of animals.

It was hard, but Janet proved true, and the Queen had to go back to Fairyland empty-handed.

Fair enough. But what did any of that have to do with my butter spirit and him planning to make me his tithe to Old Boneless?

Apparently, Miki wasn't going to tell me because she just called out the key of the first number and off she went, blasting out a tune on her accordion. In a moment, the pub was full of bobbing heads and tapping feet and I was too busy keeping up with Miki to be worrying about the relevance of old traditional ballads.

Miki was in a mood tonight. The tunes were all fast and furious, one after the other, with no time to catch a breath in between. Most of the time, when we got to the end of one of our regular sets, she'd simply call out a key signature and jump directly into the next set.

I didn't really think of it as peculiar to this particular night. Once she got on stage, you never knew where Miki would let the muse take her. Having a long-standing fondness for jazz tenor sax solos, as well as a newfound love for Mexican conjunto music that she'd picked up on our tours through Texas and the Southwest, she could as easily slide from whatever Irish tune we might be playing into a Ben Webster solo, or some norteño piece she'd picked up from a Flaco Jimenez album.

But tonight it was all hard-driving reels and we didn't come up for air until just before the end of our first set. I took the momentary respite to kill the volume on my guitar and give it a proper retuning, not really listening to what Miki was telling the audience. But I did note that they all had the same, slightly-stunned expression that I was sure I was wearing. Miki in full tear on her box could do it to anyone, and even playing on stage with her, I wasn't immune.

I got the last string in tune, then suddenly realized what Miki was telling the audience.

"…have to ask yourselves, why these stories persist," she was saying. "We've always had them and we still do. I mean, alien abductions—that's just a new twist on the old tale of people getting taken away by the fairies, isn't it? Now I don't want to go all woo-woo on you here, but tonight's one of the two nights of the year that these little buggers are given complete free rein to cause what havoc they can for us mortals. The other's on Halloween.

"Anyway," she went on, smiling brightly at the audience in that way she had that immediately made you have to smile back, "whether you believe or not, it can't hurt to wish a bit of good luck our way, right? So while we're playing this next tune, I want you to think about how everybody here should be kept safe from the influence and malice of these so-called Good Neighbours. What do you think?"

She cocked her head and gave them a goofy look which got her a round of laughter and applause.

"Key of D," she told me and launched into "The Fairies' Hornpipe."

"Remember," she said over the opening bars, directing her attention back to the audience. "Fairies bad. Us good."

I looked out at the crowd as I backed Miki up. People were still smiling, some of them clapping along to the simple rhythm of the tune. And I'd bet more than half of them were doing what she'd said, thinking protective thoughts for everybody here inside the pub.

This was Miki's big plan? I found myself thinking.

Don't get me wrong. I appreciated whatever effort she might have made to solve my problem, but this didn't seem like it would be all that effectual. And I sure didn't see the connection to that old ballad, "Tam Lin."

But then I realized that the Native women I'd noted earlier were all standing up now, backs against the various walls. One after the other, they lit smudgesticks and soon that pungent scent of herbs and twigs was drifting through the pub, only this time, except for me, nobody seemed to notice.

And then I realized something else. While the audience continued to clap and stomp away to the music, while I could still *hear* the music, I wasn't playing my guitar anymore. I looked over at Miki and there seemed to be two of her, superimposed over each other. One still playing away on that old box of hers—she'd switched to a tune that I recognized as "The Fairy Reel"; the other regarding me with a serious expression in her eyes.

The sound of her playing and the crowd was muted. Actually, my sight felt muted, too, like there was a thin gauze hanging in front of my eyes.

"It's up to you now," the Miki who wasn't playing said. "Go outside and deal with him."

"What...where *are* we?"

"In between. Not quite in the world, not quite in the otherworld where the spirits are stronger."

"I don't understand. How did you bring us here?"

"I didn't," she said. "They did."

I didn't have to ask who she meant. It was the Native women, with their smudgesticks and something else. I heard a low, rhythmical drumming, under the music, under the noise of the crowd. Mixed with it were the sounds of rattles and flutes, keeping time to Miki's tune, but following their own rhythm at the same time. I couldn't see the players.

More spirits, I guessed. But Native ones.

"And I'm not really with you," Miki added. "You're on your own."

"I don't understand—" I began, but she cut me off.

"There's not a big window of time here, Conn. Get a move on. And remember what I told you."

"I know. Think of the ballad. Why can't you just *tell* me what you've got planned?"

She smiled, but there was no humour in it. Only a kind of sadness.

"You'll know what to do when the time comes," she said. "One way or another, you can finish this business tonight."

You know how in a dream you find yourself doing things that don't make sense in retrospect, but in the dream they're perfectly logical? That's what this felt like. I got up and put my guitar in its stand, then made my way down from the stage and through the tables to the front door of the pub. No one paid the slightest attention to me except for Tommy, who gave me a smile and a thumb's up as I passed the soundboard where he was sitting.

I thought of stopping to see if he could tell me what was going on, but then I remembered Miki saying something about there not being a lot of time, so I continued on to the door. Considering how weird everything else had gotten, I didn't really expect Harnett's Point to be still waiting for me outside. But it was. And that wasn't all that was waiting for me.

I stepped out into the parking lot, then stopped dead in my tracks. Nita stood there, waiting in an open parking spot between an SUV and a Volvo stationwagon. She looked as gorgeous as ever and my heartbeat did a little skip of happiness before my chest went tight with anxiety. I looked to the left and right, searching for some sign of the butter spirit, but so far as I could tell we were alone. Which I knew meant nothing.

"Nita…" I said, stepping closer to her. "What are you *doing* here?"

The smile she'd been wearing faltered. "Your friend Miki…she asked me to come. She said we had to do this and then everything would be all right."

I shook my head. *What* had Miki been thinking?

In the light from the bar's signage behind me I could see that her eyes were already getting puffy and her nose was beginning to run—her allergy to me kicking in.

"I shouldn't have come, should I?" Nita said. "I can tell. You don't really want me here."

The sadness I saw rising up in her broke my heart.

"No, it's not that," I told her. "It's just…oh, Christ, Miki couldn't have picked a worse night to have you come."

She started to say something, but a voice to the side spoke first.

"Using words like that will just make it worse on you, Conn O'Neill."

I turned and this time I spotted him. He was perched on the roof of an old Chev two-door, one car over from the Volvo. The butter spirit with his hair like dreads and that glare in his eyes.

"I'm not afraid," Nita told me. "Miki told me all about it."

"I wish she'd told me," I said.

The butter spirit jumped onto the roof of the Volvo and grinned down at me.

"Don't know what you've got planned here, my wee boyo," he said. "I just know it's too late."

Nita and I both felt it then, a sudden coldness in the air. Looking over her shoulder, I was the first to see him: a fog lifting from the pavement of the parking lot that became the figure of a man with a cloak of wreathing mist that swirled about him. The Grey Man, his features sharp and pale, framed by long grey hair. Old Boneless himself. He didn't seem completely solid and I remembered my dad telling me how he sustained himself on the smoke from chimneys and factories, on the exhaust from cars and other machines. That had never made sense until now.

His gaze had none of the butter spirit's meanness. Instead, he appeared completely indifferent, and in him, that struck me as far more dangerous.

"Get away, girl," the butter spirit told Nita. "Or you'll suffer the same fate as your boyo."

Nita ignored him. She moved closer to me.

"H-hold me," she said.

She could barely get the words out, her allergy to me closing up her throat.

"But—" I began, but couldn't finish.

She tried to speak, only she didn't have the breath anymore. Swaying, she would have fallen if I hadn't stepped forward and taken her into my arms. I lowered her to the pavement and knelt there, holding her tight, my heart filling with hopelessness and despair.

"Let her go," the butter spirit said.

I wanted to. I knew I should get as far away from her as I could so that she could recover from this allergy attack. But Nita still had the strength to grip my arm and she wouldn't let go. I knew what she was trying to tell me. So I looked down into her face and I kissed her instead.

Her skin changed under my lips. When I lifted my head, I found myself holding a corpse. Nita's lovely brown skin had gone pallid and cold and her gaze was flat. Empty. Her lips moved and then a maggot crept out of the corner of her mouth.

I might have pushed her aside and scrambled to my feet in horror, except somehow I managed to remember Miki's cryptic reminders about the old ballad. So I held her closer. Even when the flesh fell apart in my grip and all I held were bones, attached to each other by bits of dried muscle and sinew. I held her even closer then, tenderly cradling the skull against my chest. Wisps of what had once been her thick brown hair tickled my hand.

I still didn't really see the connection between the ballad and our situation. I was the one in peril with fairy, not her. I should be the one changing shapes. But I knew I wouldn't let her go, never mind the gender-switch from the ballad.

None of this made much sense anyway, from the butter spirit's first taking affront to me, through the years of petty torment to this night, when the tithe he owed the Grey Man was due. None of it seemed real. It was all part and parcel of that same dream-like state I felt I'd entered back on the stage inside the pub. I suppose that was what let me continue to kneel here, holding the apparent remains of Nita in my arms, and still function.

"This man is yours," I heard the butter spirit say. "My tithe to you."

Before the Grey Man could do whatever it was he was going to do, I lifted my head and met his flat, expressionless gaze. I still felt disconnected, reality floundering all around me, but I knew what I needed to do. It wasn't Miki's advice I needed to take, but my dad's.

"I'm honoured to make your acquaintance, sir," I said, falling back on the formal speech patterns I remembered from dad's stories.

For the first time since he arrived, I saw a flicker of interest in the Grey Man's gaze.

"Are you now?" he said.

His voice was a voice from the grave, deep and husky, filled with cold air.

I gave a slow nod in response. I was no longer trying to figure out what Miki's plan had been. Instead, I concentrated on the stories from my dad, how in them, no matter how malevolent or kind the fairy spirit might seem to be, the one thing they all demanded of us mortals was respect.

"I am, sir," I said. "It's a rare privilege to be able to look upon one so grand as yourself."

"Even when I am here to eat your soul?"

"Even, then, sir."

"What game are you playing at?" he demanded.

"No game, sir. Though in all fairness, I feel I should tell you that your butter spirit actually has no claim to my soul. That being the case, it puzzles me how he can offer me up as his tithe to you. It seems to me—if you'll pardon my speaking out of turn like this—rather disrespectful."

The Grey Man turned that dark gaze of his to the butter spirit. "Is this true, Fardoragh Og?"

The butter spirit spat at me. "Lies, my lord. Everything he says is a lie."

"Then tell me, how did you gain a lien on his soul?"

The butter spirit couldn't find the words he needed.

"Well?"

"He...I..."

"If I might speak, sir?" I asked.

The butter spirit wanted to protest — that was easy to see — but he kept his mouth shut when the Grey Man nodded. I explained the circumstances of the butter spirit's enmity to me, and how when I'd realized my mistake, I'd tried to apologize.

"And where in this sorry tale," the Grey Man asked the butter spirit, "did you acquire the lien on this man's soul?"

"I..."

"Do you know what would have happened if I had taken it in these circumstances?"

"N-no, my lord."

"For the wrongful murder of their son, I would have been in debt to his family for eternity."

"I...I didn't...I never thought, my lord..."

"Come here, little man."

With great reluctance, the butter spirit shuffled to where the tall figure of the Grey Man stood. I didn't know what was coming next, but I knew that if I could get Nita and myself safely out of this, the last thing we'd need would be the continued enmity of the butter spirit, magnified by who knew how much after tonight's ordeal?

"Sir?" I said. "May I speak?"

The Grey Man's gaze touched me and I shivered. "Go ahead."

"It's just...this all seems to have been a series of unfortunate misunderstandings, sir. Couldn't we, perhaps, simply put it all behind us and carry on with our lives?"

"You ask for clemency toward your enemy?"

"I don't really think of him as an enemy, sir. Truly, it was just a misunderstanding that grew out proportion in the heat of the moment. And I should never have disrespected him in the first place."

The butter spirit actually gave me a grateful look, but the Grey Man appeared unmoved. He grabbed the butter spirit by the scruff of his neck.

"You offer a commendable sentiment," he told me, "but I care only for the danger he put me in. It's not something I can afford to have repeated."

With that, he pulled the little man towards him. I thought, how odd that he would embrace the butter spirit in a moment such as this. But the Grey Man didn't draw him close for an embrace, so much as to devour him. The butter spirit gave a shriek as the foggy drapes of the cloak folded over him. And then he was gone, swallowed in the cloak of fog, with only the fading echo of his cry remaining before it, too, was gone.

"Now there is only one last problem," the Grey Man said, his dark gaze returning to me.

I swallowed hard.

"I am still owed a tithe from your world," he said. "Some human artifact or spirit. But I stand before you empty-handed."

I didn't reply. What was I going to say?

"I can only think of one solution," he went on. "Will you swear fealty to me?"

I had to be careful now.

"Gladly, sir," I told him. "So long as my doing so causes no harm to any other being."

"You think I would have you do evil things?"

"Sir, I have no idea what you would want from me. I'm only being honest with you."

For a long moment the Grey Man stood there, considering me.

"I owe you a favour," he finally said. "I know you spoke up only to save your own skin, but by doing so, you prevented me from an eternity of servitude to your family."

"Sir, it was never my intention to—"

He cut me off with a sharp gesture of his hand. "Enough! You've made your point. You're very respectful. Now give it a rest." He sighed, then added, "Burn a candle for me from time to time, and we'll leave it at that."

I knew he was about to go.

"Sir," I said before he could leave. "My friend…"

He looked down at the bundle of bones in my arms, held together with sinew and dried muscle.

"It's only a glamour," he said. "Seen by you, felt by her."

And then he was gone in a swirl of fog.

I'd managed to keep my soul. The butter spirit would no longer be tormenting me. But I still knelt there with bones in my arms where Nita should be.

At that moment there came a roar of applause from inside the bar. I turned in the direction of the door. In seemed so inappropriate that they would be cheering the Grey Man's departure, but then I realized that it was only that Miki had ended her set.

I started to get to my feet, not an easy process because those bones weighed more than you'd think they would. But I refused to put them down.

I was still trying to stand when the door opened and one of those tall Native women I'd seen inside the bar came out into the parking lot. A moment later and the others followed her, one by one, nine of them in all. The last of them was an old, old woman with eyes as dark as the Grey Man's. When her gaze settled on me, I felt as nervous as I had under his attention.

"You did well," one of the younger women said — younger meaning she was in her forties. I couldn't tell how old the oldest of them was. She seemed ageless.

When they started to walk across the parking lot, I called out after them.

"Please! Can you help me with my friend?"

The old woman was the closest. She reached into her pocket and tossed what looked like a handful of pollen into the air, then blew it in my direction. I sneezed. Once. Twice. A third time. Blinked to clear my eyes.

By the time I was done, the Native women were gone. But Nita was in my arms — the real Nita, seemingly unaffected by allergies. Her eyelids fluttered and then she was looking up at me. A small smile touched her lips.

"I had the strangest dream," she said.

"It's okay. It's all over now."

"Did…did we win? she asked.

I wouldn't call it winning. I don't know what I'd call it. But at least it seemed we were free.

"Yeah," I told her, settling on the easiest reply. "We won."

5

Strong whiskey was the order of the day when we got back inside, because Lord, did I need a drink. Jameson's in glass tumblers, no ice. I had the waitress leave the bottle at the table where Nita and I sat with Miki and her friend Tommy. We still had a half hour before Miki and I had to start our next set.

"I can't believe you let me go into that so blind," I told Miki.

"Shut up and drink your whiskey."

"No, really."

"I told you why. It was so that the butter spirit wouldn't get a hint of what I had planned."

"But how could you know the Grey Man would swallow him and let me go?"

Miki shrugged. "I listened to your story, and then I talked to Nita about it. I knew the butter spirit didn't have a hold on you except for his malice. He couldn't offer you as a tithe. But if I'd mentioned it to you, he could have heard and made a different plan."

I was only half-listening, my attention now focused on the other thing that had been so troubling to me.

"And I can't believe you put Nita in that danger," I told her.

"I had to make sure you were both free of his spells. She had to be here for that. Besides, although you won't get them to admit it most of the time, the spirits are big on courage and true love. I figured with the two of you there, you'd show both."

"It's okay," Nita said, putting her hand over mine and giving it a squeeze. "Once she told me how it would go, I agreed to it."

I shook my head and used my free hand to have another sip of the whiskey. I knew I'd be playing very simple chords when we got back on stage for the next set.

"I don't even know how she got hold of you," I said.

"Oh, that was dead simple," Miki told me. "Once I knew she worked for the city's social services, it was easy to get her number."

I glanced across the table at Tommy. Of the four of us, he was the only one not drinking the whiskey. He had a ginger ale on the table in front of him.

"You don't seem much surprised by any of this," I said to him.

That seemed to be the tag-line of this whole sorry affair. Maybe I should have been more surprised by people not taking it all at face value.

He shrugged. "I grew up on the rez with the aunts. There's not much that surprises me anymore."

"I never got to thank them."

"I'll pass it on for you."

"So, are you happy?" Miki asked.

She looked from me to Nita, beaming with the look of someone who'd not only got the job done, but got it done well.

"Very," Nita assured her.

"And will you be together now?" Miki asked.

I met Nita's gaze and saw the love shining in her eyes, just as I knew it was in my own.

"Of course you are," Miki went on before we could answer. "Lord, I love a happy ending. I should go back to Ireland and take up matchmaking. It's a respectable profession there, you know," she told Tommy.

"Yeah," he said. "I saw the movie."

"What movie?"

"*The Matchmaker.*"

"Oh, please."

I gave Nita's hand a little tug and we left the two of them to go on at each other while we went outside to get a breath of air. It was a gorgeous night, the sky so full of stars that even the electric aura of the lights of Harnett's Point's couldn't put a damper on them.

"It's hard to believe we're finally free of that little bugger," I said. "I didn't think we'd ever be able to do anything but talk on the phone."

"Stop wasting time," Nita told me.

Then she wrapped her arms around my neck and drew me down for a long, deep kiss.